Fate stinks. It's a pile of shit because you've got no control over it. Basically, whatever you do you'll always get screwed. Mum says my dad walked out on us because it was written that way. Back home, we call it *mektoub*. It's like a film script and we're the actors. Trouble is, our scriptwriter's got no talent. He's never heard of happily ever after.

JUST LIKE TOMORROW

Faïza Guène

Translated from the French
by Sarah Adams

DEFINITIONS

JUST LIKE TOMORROW
A DEFINITIONS BOOK 978 1 862 30158 0 (from January 2007)
1 862 30158 1

First published in French in 2004 by
Hachette Littératures under the title *Kiffe kiffe demain*
Published in Great Britain by Definitions,
an imprint of Random House Children's Books

Hachette Littératures edition published 2004
Definitions edition published 2006

1 3 5 7 9 10 8 6 4 2

Set in New Baskerville by Palimpsest Book Production Limited,
Polmont, Stirlingshire

Definitions are published by Random House Children's Books,
61–63 Uxbridge Road, London W5 5SA,
a division of The Random House Group Ltd,
in Australia by Random House Australia (Pty) Ltd,
20 Alfred Street, Milsons Point, Sydney, NSW 2061, Australia,
in New Zealand by Random House New Zealand Ltd,
18 Poland Road, Glenfield, Auckland 10, New Zealand,
and in South Africa by Random House (Pty) Ltd,
Isle of Houghton, Corner of Boundary Road & Carse O'Gowrie,
Houghton 2198, South Africa

THE RANDOM HOUSE GROUP Limited Reg. No. 954009
www.kidsatrandomhouse.co.uk

A CIP catalogue record for this book is available from the British Library.

Printed and bound in Great Britain by
Cox & Wyman Ltd, Reading, Berkshire

For my mother and father

The translator would like to thank Cleo Soazandry and all the slangstas at *Live Magazine*.

It's Monday and, like every Monday, I've been round at Mrs Burlaud's. Mrs Burlaud is old, ugly and she smells of Quit Nits shampoo. I'd say she's harmless, but sometimes I worry. Today she took a whole load of weird pictures out of her bottom drawer. We're talking huge stains that looked like dried sick. She asked me what they made me think of. When I told her, she stared at me with her sticky-out eyes, shaking her head like one of those toy dogs in the backs of cars.

It was school that signed me up to see her. The teachers, when they weren't on strike I mean, decided I was shut down or depressed or something and needed help. Maybe they've got a point. Who gives a shit? I go, it's free.

I guess I've been like this since my dad left. He went far away. Back to Morocco, to marry another woman who's younger and more fertile than my mum. After me, Mum couldn't have any more children. But it wasn't like she didn't try. So when I think how some girls get pregnant

1

first time, without even meaning to ... Dad wanted a son. For his pride, his reputation, the family honour and probably tons of other stupid reasons. But he only got one kid, a girl. Me. Let's say I didn't exactly meet customer requirements. Trouble is, it's not like at the supermarket: he couldn't get his money back. So one day, I guess Mr How-Big-Is-My-Beard realised there was no point staying with my mum and he cleared off. Just like that, no warning or anything. I was watching an episode from the fourth series of the *X-Files* that I'd got from the video club along from our block. The door banged. From the window, I saw a grey taxi pulling out. That's all. It's been over six months. She's probably pregnant by now, that peasant woman he's married. I know exactly what happens next: seven days after the birth, they'll invite the whole village to the baptism ceremony. A band of old sheiks'll come over specially with their camel-hide drums. It'll cost him a fortune – all his worker's pension from Renault. And then they'll slit the throat of some big fat sheep, to give the baby its name. It'll be Mohammed. Ten to one.

When Mrs Burlaud asks me if I miss my dad, I say 'no', but she doesn't believe me. For an old lady she's got her eye on the ball. Whatever, it's no big deal, my mum's here. Well, when I say here, we're talking physically. Because in her head she's somewhere else you get me, like even further away than my dad.

Ramadan started just over a week ago. I got Mum to sign a slip to say I wouldn't be eating in the school canteen this term. When I gave it to the Head, he asked if I was taking him for a complete and total idiot? The Head's called Mr Loiseau. He's fat, he's stupid, and when he opens his mouth it smells of cheap wine, plus he smokes a pipe. At the end of the school day, his big sister picks him up from the main gates in a red Skoda. So he's kind of got a credibility problem when he wants to make out he's boss.

Anyway, Mr Loiseau asked me if I was taking him for a complete and total idiot because he thought I'd signed that slip instead of my mum. How stupid is that? If I'd wanted to fake her signature, I'd of written her name. Mum had just done this squiggle. She's not used to holding a biro. Bet that didn't even occur to Mr Brain-Dead-Head. He's one of those people who thinks illiteracy is like AIDS. It only happens in Africa.

Mum hasn't been working for long. She cleans at the Formula 1 Motel in Bagnolet – while she's waiting to find something else. Soon I hope. Sometimes, when she gets home late, she cries. She says it's from feeling so tired. It's worse during Ramadan, because when it's time to break the fast, around 5.30, she's still at work. So if she wants to eat, she has to hide some dried dates in her overall. She's even sewn an inside pocket to avoid attention, because if her boss saw her he'd give her a blasting.

Everyone calls her 'Fatima' at the Formula 1 in Bagnolet. They're always shouting at her, and they keep a close eye on her to check she doesn't jack anything from the bedrooms.

But Mum's name isn't Fatima, it's Yasmina. I guess Mr Schmidt must think it's *so* funny to call all the Arabs 'Fatima', all the blacks 'Mamadou' and all the Chinese 'Ping-Pong'. *Stupid bloody foreigners.*

Mr Schmidt's her supervisor. He's from the Alsace region. Sometimes, I wish he'd go rot in a basement and get eaten alive by rats. When I talk like that, Mum gives me a hard time. She says you shouldn't wish death on anybody, not even your worst enemy. One day, he was so rude to her she came home and cried her eyes out. Last time I saw someone crying that hard was when Myriam peed her pants on the school skiing trip. That bastard Schmidt thought Mum was disrespecting him because, with her accent, she pronounces his name Shit.

We've had a whole parade of social workers coming to the flat since the old man cleared out. I can't remember what the new one's called, but it's something like Dubois or Dupont or Dupré, a name that tells you she's from somewhere *nice*, you get me. I think she's a fool, plus she's always smiling for no reason. Like even when she's not meant to. You'd think she needs to do other people's happiness for them. Once she asked if I wanted us to be friends. I said no way. But I guess I messed up, because you should of seen the look my mum gave me. She was probably scared our benefits would get cut if I didn't suck up to their stupid social worker.

Before Mrs Wotsit, we had a man. Yep, a male. He worked for the council and looked like Laurent Cabrol, that guy who used to host *Heroes' Night* on Channel 1. Shame it's finished. These days, Laurent Cabrol's on page 30 of *TV Mag*, right at the bottom of the page in the corner, doing an ad for central heating in a yellow and black striped T-shirt. Anyway, the social worker was his spitting image. Total opposite to Mrs Thingumyjig. He never cracked a joke, never smiled and he dressed like Professor Calculus from *Tintin*. Once he told my mum he'd been doing this job for ten years, and it was the first time he'd seen *people like us with a one-child family*. He was probably thinking 'Arabs', but he didn't say so. Coming round to our place was like an exotic experience for him. He kept shooting weird looks at all the knick-knacks we've got on display, the ones my mum brought over from Morocco after she got married. Seeing as we wear *babouches* at home, he reckoned he was doing the right thing taking off his shoes when he walked into the flat. Except he'd got monster feet. His second toe was at least ten times longer than his big one. It looked like he was giving the V-sign inside his socks. Plus they stank. He pretended he cared, but he was just bluffing. It was all a front. He didn't give a shit about us. Then he quit. I heard he moved to the country-side. For all I know he retrained as a cheese-maker. He probably drives around the villages of old-skool France in his sky-blue van after Mass on Sundays selling rye bread, Roquefort cheese and *saucisson sec*.

I think Mrs Thingumybob's a fool, but at least

she does a better job of playing social worker to the needy. She really makes out she cares about our lives. Sometimes, you'd almost believe her. She fires questions at me in that high-pitched voice she's got. The other day, she wanted to know what I'd been reading recently. I shrugged. Matter of fact, I've just finished this Moroccan novel called *The Sand Child* by Tahar Ben Jelloun. It's about a little girl who got brought up as a boy because she was the eighth daughter in the family and her father wanted a son. Plus, at the time when it was set, you didn't have ultrasound or contraception. No kids on sale or return, you get me.

Fate stinks. It's a pile of shit because you've got no control over it. Basically, whatever you do you'll always get screwed. Mum says my dad walked out on us because it was written that way. Back home, we call it *mektoub*. It's like a film script and we're the actors. Trouble is, our scriptwriter's got no talent. He's never heard of happily ever after.

My mum thought France was like in those black and white films from the sixties. The ones where the buff actor's always telling his woman so much lies, with a cigarette dangling from his lips. My mum and her cousin Bouchra had found a way of picking up French TV with the aerial they'd rigged from a stainless steel couscous-maker. So when she and my dad turned up in the Paris suburb of Livry-Gargan, February 1984, she thought they must of caught the wrong boat and got the wrong country. She told me the first thing she did when she walked into our tiny two-room flat was throw up. I wonder whether it was the seasickness or a seventh sense warning her about life in these ends.

The last time we went back to Morocco, it did my head in. There were these old women with tattoos who kept coming over and sitting next to Mum at the weddings and baptisms and circumcision ceremonies.

'A word in your ear, Yasmina. Your girl's

growing up into a young woman, it's time you thought about finding her a boy from a good family. What about Rachid, that nice young welder?'

Stupid cows. I know exactly who they were on about. Everyone calls him 'Mule-head Rachid'. Even the six-year-olds are always winding him up and laughing in his face. Plus he's missing four teeth, he can't read, he squints and he stinks of piss. Back over there, as long as you've got two grape-pips for boobs, you shut up when you're told to and you know how to bake bread, then bam you're a catch. Except I don't think we'll ever go back to Morocco now. We can't afford it for one thing, plus my mum says she'd feel ashamed, big time. People would point at her. She thinks it's her fault, what happened. I'd say there are two guilty parties in this story: my dad and fate.

We worry about the future but what's the point? We might not even have one. We could die in ten days, or tomorrow or right here and now. You don't find out ahead of time. There's no advance warning, no final reminder. It's not like when your electricity bill's overdue. That's how it was with Mr Rodriguez, my neighbour from the second floor, the one who fought in the war for real. He died not long ago. Yeah, OK, so he was old, but still, we weren't expecting it.

Sometimes I think about death. I've even had dreams about it. One night, I was at my own funeral. Hardly anyone there. Just my mum, Mrs Burlaud, Carla the Portuguese lady who cleans the lifts in our block, Leonardo DiCaprio from *Titanic* and my friend Sarah who moved to Trappes when I was twelve. My dad wasn't there. He had to look after that pregnant peasant and his Momo-to-be while I was, well, dead. Makes you sick. Bet his son's even thicker than Rachid the welder. I hope he limps and has problems with his eyesight, and that when he hits puberty he has a massive acne attack. There won't be any Biactol or Clearasil for his spots in their arse-end-of-nowhere village. Except maybe on the black market, if he can play the system. Whichever way you look at it, he'll be a dud, that's for sure. In this family, being a fool is passed down from father to son. When he's sixteen, he'll sell potatoes and turnips at the market. And on his way back home, on his black mule, he'll kid himself: 'I'm a glamorous kind of guy.'

I'd like to work in something glamorous later on. Don't know what exactly . . . Trouble is, I'm rubbish at school. The only subject where they don't fail me straight off is Art and Design. It's better than nothing, but I don't reckon sticking leaves onto drawing paper is going to be a big help for my future. I just don't want to end up behind a fast food counter, smiling all the time and asking customers: 'Drink? Regular or large? Eat in or to go? For or against abortion?' And getting blasted by my supervisor if I serve a customer too many fries because he smiled at me. You never know, could of been the man of my dreams. I'd give him a reduction, he'd take me out for a meal at the Hippopotamus Steak House, ask me to marry him, and we'd live happily ever after in his five-room, to-die-for flat.

Our Child Benefit book came through. Just in time. Now I won't have to go to the big Red Cross in town. How embarrassing is that? Once, me and my mum ran into Nacera the Witch at the main entrance. She's this woman we've known since back in the day. Mum borrows money from her when we're totally broke. I hate her. She only remembers we owe her dough when there's *this* many people around, just to embarrass my mum. So, we run into Nacera at the main entrance to the Red Cross. Mum's squirming, but this other woman's lapping it up.

'So, Yasmina, you've come to the Red Cross to . . . collect something?'

'Yes.'

'And I've come to . . . donate!'

'May God reward you.'

Grrr . . . I hope God rewards her with zilch apart from staying an ugly old cow. We went back home without choosing anything, because Mum didn't want to pick clothes that could of belonged to the witch. It'd just give her another excuse to open her fat mouth, like: 'Well I never, I believe that's *my* skirt you're wearing.' I was proud of my mum. That's dignity for you, the kind they don't teach you at school.

Talking of school, I've got to do this homework assignment for Citizenship Studies. It's about respect. Mr Werbert gave it to us. He's an OK teacher, but I'm not keen on him talking to me, because it's like he's sorry for me or something. It reminds me of when Mum and me ask the old woman at the Red Cross for a plastic bag to put our sweaters in and she looks at us all misty-eyed. Each time, we're this close to handing back her sweaters and clearing out. Mr Werbert's the same. He makes out he's some kind of people's prophet. Keeps telling me I can have an appointment to see him, if I need to . . . But it's just so he can feel good about himself, and tell his mates in a trendy Paris bar how challenging it is teaching in the 'at risk' schools in the suburbs. Yuk.

So what am I going to say about respect? It's not like the teachers give a shit about our essays. Bet you they don't even read them. Just give you any old mark, stuff them in their work bags and go back to lounging on their leather settee, between their two kids, Pamela, aged ten, who's playing *Dishwasher Barbie*, and Brandon, twelve, who's busy eating his bogeys. Not forgetting wifey Marie-Hélène, who's just ordered a takeout because she's feeling too lazy to cook, and is reading an article about waxing your legs in *Woman Today*. Now there's disrespect for you. Waxing hurts, and if you hurt somebody it shows a lack of respect.

Whatever, I want to stop going. I've had it with school. It's bare boring, plus it's not like I speak to anyone. There's only two people I can talk to for real. Mrs Burlaud and Hamoudi. Hamoudi's one of the main guys on the estate. Must be about twenty-eight. He spends his days hanging out around the entrances to the tower blocks and, like he's always reminding me, he's known me since I was 'smaller than a block of hash'.

Hamoudi smokes a lot of spliffs. He's always high, and maybe that's why I like him. Neither of us rates our reality, you get me. Sometimes, when I'm on my way back from the shops, he stops me on the ground floor to talk about stuff. 'Just five minutes,' he says, but we end up talking for an hour or even two. Well, *he* does mostly. A lot of times he recites these poems by Arthur Rimbaud. Or what he can remember of them, because the thing about hash is it mashes your memory. But when he does them for me with his accent and hand actions coming from the street, even if I don't catch all the meaning, they seem kind of beautiful to me.

It's too bad he didn't finish school. It's because of prison. He told me his crew got him mixed up in some kind of business, but he won't tell me what – 'You're underage, innit.' When he got out, he dropped everything even though he'd nearly gone all the way with his studies. Like he nearly finished college! So when I see the police frisking Hamoudi near our main entrance or I hear them bad-mouthing him with stuff like 'shit-head', or 'piece of scum', I tell myself they don't know anything about poetry. If Hamoudi was a bit older, I'd like it if he'd been my dad. We talked for the longest time when he found out what happened to me and my mum. 'Family's sacred, man,' he said, rolling his billionth joint. He should know: he's got eight brothers and sisters and most of them are married. But Hamoudi says he's not into marriage. What's the point? It's another headache, like we haven't got enough to deal with already. He's right. Except I haven't really got a family any more. We're just a half-family now.

I was bored, so I took the Metro. I didn't know where to go, but it's a way of passing the time. I like seeing so many different faces. I did all of Line 5, from end to end.

At one of the early stops, this Romanian guy in a fake leather jacket and a grey hat gets on. He's got this old accordion that's so manky there's dust all over the keys that never got used, and he's playing these old tunes, the kind you hear in arty French films or on those boring late-night documentaries. He did a nice job of cheering up the journey. I even spotted the blue rinses in the carriage, like the really uptight ones, tapping their toes on the sly. And get this, the gypsy guy accompanied each movement of his instrument with a sway of his head, and when he smiled he flashed all his teeth, or the ones he'd got left. His face was straight out of a cartoon, a bit like the cat in *Alice in Wonderland*.

I had a great time imagining him living in a caravan, being descended from a dynasty of nomads who'd travelled across many lands and setting up makeshift camp on a patch of wasteland outside Paris with his pretty wife called Lucia (like that brand of mozzarella) who had stunning curly black hair down to her waist. Bet they got married on a big empty beach in Spain, around a massive fire with big red flames that danced against the black night sky. Or that's how I saw it. Anyway, I followed him each time he switched compartments, to get the most out of his magic accordion. But then talk about die of shame. He was heading my way, holding out his McDonald's paper cup full of loose change and, well, I didn't have anything to give him. So I went for this cheap trick, the kind of thing tight-fisted bastards normally do. As soon as he got to me, I looked the other way, as in 'I'm watching what's happening on the opposite platform'. Except, big surprise, there wasn't anything happening on the opposite platform.

If I win the Lottery on Wednesday, I'll get him a swanky caravan, with loads of gizmos, the best-looking one on the campsite I'm telling you. Like in the Sunday night showcase for *The Price is Right*.

Then I'll buy myself some new winter gloves, with no holes, because the cold air gets into my ones. There's a major gap in the middle finger of the left hand. It's going to be a problem one of these days . . .

Next, I'll take Mum to have a manicure, seeing how that's what she was talking about last time with Mrs Wotsit, the social worker, except my mum didn't even know what a manicure was. She was looking at her nails that are ruined by all those *made in Chernobyl* cleaning products, and comparing them to Mrs Thingumyjig's who couldn't help showing off because her nails were like *this* clean, *this* filed, *this* polished. She even rubbed the corner of her eye with her little finger, and her mouth was ever so slightly open, like those girls you see applying their mascara on telly. Just to gloat and make my mum, who didn't even know what a manicure was, notice her perfect nails. I wanted to rip them out, one by one.

So anyway, when I got out of the Metro, I passed two Pakistani guys selling hot chestnuts and roasted peanuts. They kept saying the same thing, over and over again: 'Hot chestnuts and roasted peanuts to warm you up!' Except they didn't just say it, they kind of chanted it almost like a song, in their Pakistani accents. I couldn't get those lyrics out of my head. That evening, when I got back home, I ended up singing them while I was cooking Mum her rice.

On Friday Mum and me were invited round to Aunt Zohra's to eat her couscous. We caught an early train, so we could spend the whole day round at hers. It's been a long time since we've been asked anywhere.

Aunt Zohra isn't my real aunt, but seeing as she's known Mum for the longest time I've got into the habit of calling her that. Before, they used to go to sewing class together. Then Aunt Zohra moved to Mantes-la-Jolie. Mum signed up for the sewing lessons, she told me, because nearly all the women there were *Maghrébines* from back home, and those Wednesday afternoon sessions round Singer sewing machines from the 1980s reminded her of the *bled*.

Aunt Zohra's got big green eyes and she laughs all the time. She's Western Algerian, from a region called Tlemcen. She's got a funny history too, because she was born on 5 July 1962, Algerian Independence Day. She was a symbol of freedom in her village for years. A lucky-

25

charm baby. That's why she's called Zohra. It means 'luck' in Arabic.

I like her because she's a real woman. A strong woman, you get me. Her husband's a retired construction worker and he's got a second wife back home, so he spends six months over there and six months back in France. Is this turning into a fashion, or what? It's like, when they retire, they all decide to make a new life for themselves and marry a younger woman. The difference is, Aunt Zohra's husband knew how to get the balance right. He does it part-time.

It doesn't seem to bother Aunt Zohra that she only sees her husband six months out of twelve. She says she gets along just fine without him, knows how to entertain herself. And once she laughed and told Mum that a man his age wasn't any use to her anyway. I didn't quite get it at first. Then I worked it out.

I hung out with Aunt Zohra's sons, Reda, Hamza and Youssef. They were mostly playing computer games. The kind you see in TV reports on 'youth and violence'. The idea was to drive the car as fast as you could while knocking over as many pedestrians as possible, and you got bonus points if they were kids or old ladies . . . I've known the boys since I was little, but I don't talk to them much any more so it was a bit tense. We didn't really know what to say. In the end they wound me up about it. Said I was like Bernardo in *Zorro*, the short one who seems a total idiot because he has this series of signs to warn Zorro if there's any danger. He's actually dumb, poor guy.

At one point, I caught the end of what Mum and Aunt Zohra were saying about my dad. Mum was telling her he wouldn't go to heaven because of what he'd done to his daughter. The way I see it, he won't be going because of what he's done to Mum. The bouncer in Paradise won't let him in. He'll send him packing, straight up. It gets on my nerves they're still talking about him. He's not here any more. We've just got to forget him.

The chickpeas are what's special about Aunt Zohra's couscous, that and the delicate way she cooks the grains. Aunt Zohra cracks me up. She's been living in France for more than twenty years and she still talks like she stepped off the plane at Paris-Orly airport a week ago.

Once, way back, she was telling Mum how she'd signed Hamza up for 'carrots'. Mum didn't have a clue what she was talking about. Then a few days later, she started giggling. She'd realised Aunt Zohra meant *karate* . . . Even her sons tease her. They say she does re-mixes of Molière's great French language. They've tagged her 'DJ Zozo'.

When it got to the end of the day, Youssef drove us back in the car. He had rap playing and nobody said a single word the whole journey. I could see Mum was thinking about something. She had turned away and was staring out the window. When we stopped, she just looked blankly at the red light. Her head was somewhere else.

Youssef drives fast. He's tall and very good-looking. When we were small, we went to the same primary school, and he always stood up for me. I didn't have a brother and he was 'one of the big boys in Year 6'. I remember we did that campaign together called 'A Grain of Rice can Save a Life'. It was when there was the famine in Somalia back in the nineties. He made me believe the slogan was for real, like for every grain of rice we sent over we really saved a life. I was *this* proud of saving so many lives with the 500g bag of rice Mum bought me from Casino. It was even like I was going to count each grain of rice in the packet to be absolutely sure that, thanks to me, there were loads of Somalians who wouldn't die of hunger. I thought I was Wonderwoman. But he was bluffing me. Matter of fact, I'm still annoyed with him. Now I come to think of it, I never even found out if my bag of rice got there.

When we got to our block, Mum thanked Youssef and he set off again. The caretaker doesn't give a shit about our flats. Luckily Carla, the Portuguese cleaning lady, sometimes does her job. But when she doesn't come, it stays disgusting for weeks, and that's how it's been lately. There was piss and spit in the lift, plus it stank, but at least it was working. Luckily for us we know which buttons are for which floors, because the display panel's all scratched and melted. Someone must of got out their cigarette lighter.

The caretaker's meant to be racist. That's what Hamoudi told me. I wouldn't know, I've never spoken to him. He scares me. He's always frowning, so he's got these two lines sticking up in the middle of his forehead, like the number eleven.

Hamoudi was telling me how, back in the day, before he was caretaker of our blocks, he fought in the war in Aunt Zohra's country, in Algeria. Maybe that's why he hasn't got any earlobes and his left thumb's missing. I don't think the war's completely over for him yet, and I guess the same goes for lots of other people in this country.

29

Oh my days, Mrs Burlaud's just suggested something weird: a skiing holiday organised by some community scheme. She kept banging on about how good it would be for me. I'd meet lots of new people, have a break from this neighbourhood . . . I think it's meant to help me open up, or something.

I don't want to go because I don't fancy leaving my mum on her own, even if it's only a week. Plus we're talking a group holiday, and I can't choose the people I'm with, so forget it. You wouldn't get me anywhere near that journey. Eight hours in a bus that stinks of puke, singing songs from the eighties, with toilet breaks every half-hour, you've got to be kidding.

To start with, Mrs Burlaud thought I didn't want to go because of the money.

'You know how it works, we've already talked about that. It won't cost your mum anything, if that's what's worrying you.'

Whatever, skiing stinks of shit. It's like tobog-

31

ganing except standing up, with a silly hat and a big fat fluorescent boiler suit. I know, I've watched ski competitions on telly.

I bet Mrs Burlaud goes on a skiing holiday every winter, and I bet she never does any skiing either. Just flaunts it on the terraces, sipping hot chocolate in a pink bobble hat, while her husband takes photos with a disposable camera. Come to think of it, has she even got a husband? Never thought about that before. That's what gets me about psychologists, psychiatrists, psycho-analysts and most jobs starting with 'psy' . . . They expect you to tell them your life story, but what do they ever say about themselves? Mrs Burlaud knows stuff about me I don't even know. It makes you not want to talk to them any more. It's just a con.

Our social worker though, she's like, any excuse to tell you her life story. I found out through Mum she's getting married. And I'm like why did she need to tell her that? What's it got to do with us? OK, so she's jammy, we get the picture, no need to make such a big deal about it. Still, at least she'll have a reason for smiling the whole time. Perhaps she won't get on my nerves so much.

Yeah, all right, maybe I'm jealous. When I was little, I used to cut the hair off Barbie dolls because they were blonde. I snipped their boobs off too because I hadn't got any. Except they weren't even real Barbies. They were that poor people's brand my mum bought me at Giga Store. Spastic dolls. You played with them two days, then they looked like landmine victims. Even their first name was shit: Frances. I mean, you're not going to encourage little girls to dream with a name like that. Frances, the doll for girls without any dreams.

When I was younger, I fantasised about marrying the kind of guy who'd make everybody else look totally useless. I wasn't interested in normal men who take two months to put up a flat-pack shelf or finish a 25-piece puzzle with '5 years plus' on the box. I fancied myself with an action hero like MacGyver. A guy who can unblock your loo with a Coke can, mend the telly with a biro and blow-dry your hair with his breath. We're talking a human Swiss Army penknife.

I'm picturing a big fat wedding with the whole works. A white dress with tons of lace, a *nice* veil and a train that's at least fifteen metres long. There'd be flowers and white candles. I'd have Hamoudi for my witness, and the bridesmaids would be those three little sisters from the Ivory Coast who're always playing with their skipping rope outside our block.

Trouble is, I'm supposed to be led down the aisle by my old man. Seeing as he won't be there, we'll have to call the whole thing off. The guests'll take back their wedding presents and jack loads of food from the buffet. But where's the point? Before you start thinking about the wedding you've got to find a husband.

Our generation's lucky because you get to choose who you're going to be in love with for the rest of your life. Or the rest of the year, depending on the couple. In *Forbidden Zone*, Bernard de La Villardière was talking about divorce. He was explaining how it was on the up. Only reason I can see for this trend is *The Young and the Restless*. All the people in that TV series have been married to each other at least once, if not twice. The storylines are crazy and my mum's been following every twist in the plot since 1989. All the mums on the estate are totally into it. They meet up in the square to get the low-down on episodes they missed. We're talking worse than our boy band phase. I remember a friend giving me a poster of Filip from *2 Be 3* she'd cut out of a magazine. I was so happy, I stuck it on my bedroom wall. Filip was fit, you get me, his teeth were so white you could almost see through them, and his six-pack was straight out of a cartoon. That evening, my dad came into my bedroom. He went mad and started ripping down the poster, shouting, 'I won't have this muck under my roof, it's the devil's work! This is Satan!' I hadn't pictured the devil looking like that, but there you go ... There was just a tiny scrap of poster left on my bare wall, showing Filip's right nipple.

On the school front, term's ended as badly as it began. It's lucky my mum can't read. I mean, lucky because of my school report . . . If there's one thing that gets on my nerves, it's teachers competing to write the most original comment about a student. Result: they *all* end up sounding moronic. The worst I ever got was from Nadine Benbarchiche, our physics and chemistry teacher, who wrote: 'Distressing, a lost cause, the kind of student who makes you want to resign or commit suicide.' I guess she thought she was being funny. But I'm telling you, she was out of order. Yeah OK, so I'm a no-hoper, but she went too far. Anyway, why would I care about what she thinks? She wears a thong. So, the kind of comments I keep getting, let's call them 'ongoing themes', are things like: 'appears to be lost' or 'appears to be somewhere else' or, even worse, stuff to make you cringe: 'Earth calling planet Mars!' The only teacher to write anything nice was Mrs Lemoine, the Drawing, sorry, 'Art and Design' teacher. She came up with: 'Malleable skills.' OK, so it doesn't mean anything, but still, it was nice of her.

Seeing as my malleable skills don't count for much, a friend of Mum's suggested her son comes round to help me with my homework. According to her I'll get top marks because her son Nabil's a genius. I pointed out most Arab mums think that way about their sons. But Nabil's mum's hard-core. She reckons he's the Einstein of the tower blocks, and she's always banging on about it. He's full of it, just because he wears glasses and knows a thing or two about politics. Like, he's probably got a vague idea what the difference is between right and left. Luckily, my mum didn't exactly say yes. She played that wild card, AKA 'insh'Allah'. It doesn't mean yes or no. The proper transla-tion is 'God willing'. Thing is, you never find out if God's willing or not . . .

Nabil's a neek. He's got acne and he used to be bullied at his last school, like nearly every day. They'd take his snack at break time. We're talking a big fat loser. Me, I prefer heroes, like in the movies, the kind girls go mushy over . . . Take Al Pacino, bet you nobody jacked his snacks. You do, he pulls out his semi-automatic, blows your thumb off. No more sucking that at night before you drop off to sleep. Period.

So, for the past few weeks, Nabil's been coming round to mine on and off, to help me with my homework. The guy talks about himself too much. Thinks he knows it all. Last time, he laughed in my face because I thought Voltaire's *Zadig* was a brand of car tyre. He went on laughing for like nearly an hour, just because of that . . . At one point, seeing I'm not joining in, he says, 'Nah, no worries, I'm only kidding, it's not such a big deal. You see, in this life there's intellectuals, and then there's everyone else.' How dare him. No wonder his mum off-loaded him onto me. She just wanted to get rid of him . . .

Still, I guess I've got to take Nabil's circum-stances into account, seeing as how it can't be easy dealing with a mum like his every day. She's always on his case. I thought Nabil's name was 'Myzon' to begin with, because that's what she kept calling him every time she stroked his head. Word is, she watches over him like her life depends on it, wants to know everything about his girlfriends, his private life, etc. Yeah, OK, so he hasn't got a private life, but still, it's out of order. When he was little, she'd even turn up at break-time to hand him *petit beurre* biscuits through the school railings. Everyone on the estate says his mum's the dad round their place, and they're always taking the piss. 'Hey, Nabil! Your dad does the washing-up, innit! Does your mum wears the boxers?'

As you'll of noticed, I'm acting like one of those attorneys in American films. When it comes to defending their client who's a serial killer, rapist and cannibal, they tell you all about his dreadfully deprived childhood. That way, the members of the jury feel sorry for him and forget about sixteen-year-old Olivia's thigh still being in his freezer . . .

The way I see it, Nabil should be a lot nicer to other people. Seeing how his mum messed up his life big time and made him read Jesus' biography aged eleven.

I don't know if I'll want kids later. But I'd never make them read Jesus's life story, or say hello to old people if they didn't want to, or finish their plate.

Having kids is a big IF anyway, because in Year 8 our biology teacher showed us a birth front-on and it totally turned me off procreation.

I talked about it with Mrs Burlaud last Monday, but she was acting odd that session. She wasn't listening properly. Looked like she had something on her mind. I wonder if *she's* seeing a shrink. She should, it'd be good for her.

She's really losing it these days. She gets me

to play with Plasticine. The shapes I make don't look like anything, but she smiles:

'Yes, right, that's interesting!'

'That's interesting' doesn't mean anything. Something rubbish can be interesting for its trashiness. It's about bluffing again. That's partly what I like about Mrs Burlaud, though: she never judges you. She always takes you seriously, even when you're making a tower block out of purple Plasticine.

Then we talked about something new that's happened to me. I've got my period. Basically, I was behind compared to the other girls. The school nurse told me it was hereditary. Hereditary means it's your mum's fault. Mum got hers when she was about fifteen too. Must of been a nightmare for her, because back in the *bled* they didn't even have sanitary towels. Before, I used to think periods were blue, like in the Always advert, the one where they talk about menstrual flow and absorbency, and it always comes on while we're eating.

Mrs Burlaud asked me loads of questions. It's like she's got a thing about periods. Didn't she ever have her own or what?

She told me loads of girls freaked out the first time they started bleeding. And then she explained how periods were only the beginning.

41

I'm going to get chest pains because of my breasts growing, and I'll probably have spots on my face too. Nice. Why not greasy hair, lanky body and dark circles round my eyes like every other teenager, while we're at it? Sooner jump out of my tower block window, thanks.

I've noticed how people always make themselves feel better by looking at others who are worse off. So, that evening, I cheered myself up by thinking about poor Nabil.

When it comes to the Livry-Gargan summer festival, everybody starts getting ready ahead of time. Parents, kids, but mostly the neighbourhood gossips because the street party's great for stocking up on scandal. There were loads of stalls with mint tea and cakes, barbecued *merguez* with fries cooked by Elie the community coordinator, plus a stage with bands taking it in turns to play. Kids from the estates came to rap. They even had some girls singing with them. Yeah, OK, so the girls only came in for two stupid lines of the chorus and the rest of the time they were just stuck there, waddling about waving their arms in the air. Still, I guess it's something. One more step towards equality . . .

Mum made me have a go at the fishing stall. I did it to keep her happy, but it was the pits. Average age of the other players: 7.3 years. And the only prize I managed to fish was a one-eyed rag doll with freckles. I was bare embarrassed.

Afterwards, Mum and me headed to see Cheb

Momo. He's been singing at the Livry-Gargan summer event every year since 1987 with the same musician, same synthesiser and, you guessed it, same songs. It's not so bad because everybody ends up knowing all the words by heart, even if you don't speak a word of Arabic. Plus, what's good about Cheb Momo is everything's for real, like his black jacket with gold sequins. He makes out he's a buff thing and it works. Every year, all the mums on the estate go crazy for him.

I bumped into Hamoudi at the festival. I was going over to say hello when I noticed he was with a girl. I smiled at her the way you're meant to, like I was really happy to meet her, except I wasn't, not one little bit. Hamoudi grinned at me with his lousy teeth and said:

'Doria, er . . . this is Karine . . . and, er . . . Karine, this is Doria . . .'

He said it like he was stupid or something, and had got thirty years older overnight. Plus, he was wearing a Hawaiian shirt and it was ugly.

It felt like we were in a scene out of a Sunday soap on one of the cable channels. I was kind of upset. So I looked at the girl and went:

'See you, Karim . . .'

I didn't even realise what I was saying. They stared at me. Both looking like Pokémon.

I went back to see Mum and, for the first time, we stayed through to the end. All the other years, Dad would come and pick us up. He didn't like the idea of us hanging around. I used to watch the end of the party from our living room window.

The story with Hamoudi got me sad. I'd been worried because I hadn't seen him for the longest time. I'd even talked about him to Mrs Burlaud. And then he goes and turns up at the festival with a dumb blonde who's got a boy's name and wobbles around on fifteen-inch heels. When I went to bed that night, my head was full of sad music, like in those life insurance ads. And another thing, Hamoudi had shaved, he smelled of lavender air-freshener and his eyes weren't even bloodshot. It wasn't him. That fruitcake of a Karim's gone and totally changed him. For all I know, she's worked black magic, because I'm not feeling her right. Plus, with all that pancake foundation, she looks dodgy if you ask me.

Mum's told me bare scary stories about witch-craft back in Morocco. When she was a girl, one of her neighbours had a curse put on her at the souk, like a month before she was meant to get married. Next thing you know, she goes bald and the wedding's off. Gotta watch out. It can happen to anybody. Thinking about it, we've all got somebody who might have something against us ... Maybe Mrs Burlaud's jinxed her felt-tip pens and Plasticine so I'll have problems for the rest of my life, and that way I'll have to keep on seeing her every Monday at half past four till the day I die.

Which reminds me of something. Last year, I used to collect those witch-doctor leaflets, the ones handed out by Hindus at the top of the stairs when you're coming out of the Metro. Normal people collect stamps or postcards or corks. I collect witch-doctor propaganda.

MR KABA
International experience and reputation.
Honest, efficient, fast, discreet.

Solves every kind of problem, strengthens and encourages feelings of affection, love, consideration, fidelity between spouses, social status, driving licence, luck, success ...

Visiting times daily between 8am and 9pm
Results are not guaranteed – first appointment:
35 euros

I'm thinking if it was true, we'd all be happy, and people like Mrs Burlaud or Mrs Wotsit from the council, they'd all be unemployed.

Bet you that dumb blonde Karine goes to see weirdos like Mr Kaba. She's the wrong kind of girl for Hamoudi, because now he looks like those squeaky clean door-to-door encyclopaedia salesmen, you get me, with loads of hair gel. I know what Hamoudi's like. And being squeaky clean doesn't suit him.

When I went to bed, I took out one of the books I found in a box of rubbish outside our block. Trashy books I'd never normally read. Schmaltzy Barbara Cartland style, but bottom of the range and with a cringe-factor cover: a couple locked in a moronic embrace against a dream backdrop, just like in the brochures for Tati Holidays. Thing about a book like that is, if you want to read it on public transport, you'd better cover it with brown paper first, or fat Philip who's reading the *Figaro*, smug as hell with this aren't-I-just-so-superior pout, might just laugh in your face. The one I picked out was called *Love at First Sight in the Sahara* and, OK, so I stayed up late to finish it. The story's about this desert nomad called Steve – even this early on you know they're joking you – and Steve rescues a young red-haired teacher who's on holiday and gets mashed in an accident with her camel. The guy's got a body like mule-head Rachid except he's called Steve, but that doesn't seem to bother her. So she falls in love with a stranger she's only just met in the sand dunes. It's so stupid, you don't believe it for a second, there isn't a single original line, but you still fall for it. You even end up identifying with this total basket case who's running a high fever and keeps hallucinating because she's fallen off her camel.

Yesterday, when I went to pay the rent for Mum, the caretaker's wife – the one who got a perm in 1974 and it's still going strong – told me there's this new tenant on the estate and she's looking for a babysitter for her little girl. She said if I was interested, I could go round and see her.

'Wouldn't you like to earn a bit of pocket money?'

It's nice of her to think of me. I mean it, she could of suggested it to any of the girls from round here, but no, she thought of me. I take back everything I said about her, the perm and all that stuff . . .

'That way, you'll be able to dress like other young people your age, won't you?'

I didn't know how to take it. Nearly had a nosebleed. Even this fossil of a caretaker's wife is laughing in my face. If I'd wanted to, I could of sent that remark flying straight back where it came from. But, like a fool, I just went:

'Yeah, thanks, I'll look her up, bye!'

'Wait a minute, you're six centimes short, I can't stamp your rent book.'

Stupid old cow. But at the same time I was thinking how it'd be like safe to earn some cash anyway. We'd never be six centimes short on the rent again.

Anyway, the lady looking for a babysitter's called Lila and she's thirty. Don't know why, but I was imagining her older. Pictured her working at a department store like Galeries Lafayette, with loads of ready-made meals in her freezer. Turns out she's a cashier at Continent supermarket in Bondy and she likes cooking. She wears this thin, evenly applied eyeliner, she's got pretty brown hair that sticks up, a beautiful smile and a southern accent because she grew up in Marseilles. And another thing, she reads a whole pile of women's magazines with bullshit tests like: 'Are you the possessive type?' or 'What's Your Seduction Style?'

We didn't even spend half an hour together. She asked me a few questions and then said in any case it was written all over my face, I was a good person. So she introduced me to her daughter, Sarah. She's four but she looks kind of mature. She's clever and she's very cute, and that's something coming from me because normally with kids . . .

Lila recently split up from Sarah's dad. That's why she moved to this area. She talked a bit about what happened. You could see the hurt in her eyes. He must of taken everything. Even her favourite compilation CDs stashed away in her top drawer.

'Does three euros an hour sound OK to you?'

She just came out with it, I wasn't expecting it or anything. Thing is, she was embarrassed because she didn't think three euros was a lot, but it was all she could afford for now. She didn't realise how for me, three euros an hour is like *bare dough*. So I just went:

'Yeah, that's OK. Thanks.'

And it was a real thank you, like when you mean it, and you're happy and your eyes are stinging with tears.

I've got to pick up Sarah from the play-scheme at half past five and look after her till Lila gets back. I'd like to tell Hamoudi, but I don't see him any more. Guess he's with that fool of a Karine, playing Cluedo in her *made in Ikea* living room.

When I told Mum I was going to do some babysitting, she wasn't too happy about it. She said she could look after us all by herself, provide for us and that . . . She was on the verge of tears. We didn't say a word at supper. It wasn't like in the films. It was like in real life. And even if she agreed to it afterwards, I could tell it was still bugging her.

The shit's hitting the fan at the Formula 1 Motel in Bagnolet. Loads of Mum's co-workers are on strike. They've sorted something out with the unions so their demands get a hearing.

The woman in charge of the strike is called Fatouma Konaré, and Mum gets on with her. She told me how, at the beginning, she thought *Fatoumakonaré* was her first name and it seemed like a long one ... Fatouma started working at the Bagnolet motel in 1991. Back in the day when I couldn't even tie my own shoelaces. She was the person who started making a noise about the women workers being exploited. Mum told me she'd like to go on strike with the girls from the motel, but she can't. Fatouma and the others, they've got their husbands to help them, but we're on our own. Result: seeing as most of the other cleaners are on strike, Mum's got a thousand times more work.

Mr Schmidt, that bastard boss, must be this pissed off. Serves him right. Mum told me he's already fired quite a few of the cleaners for striking, even though he's got no right. He's sacked this Vietnamese woman on the same rota as Mum, and on a fake charge too. It makes you sick. He'll go straight to hell and it's going to hurt. He'll be waving his arms about and shouting: 'It's hot! I'm burning in here!' Who knows, in his private life Mr Schmidt could be a nice guy who spends his time smiling, donating to charity and bawling out people who park in the handicapped spaces in supermarket car parks.

Maybe she's got a point, Mrs Burlaud, when she says I hate being judged but that I do it all the time to other people. Thing is, when it comes to Mr Schmidt, there's the tiniest margin for error when I call him a bastard.

At school, they're on strike too. It's like everything's stopped around me. It's only been a few days but it seems for ever. Mr Loiseau, the Head, got attacked in the corridors by a student from outside. I wasn't there, but word is this guy blasted Mr Loiseau in the face with a tear gas canister. You've got to admit he's unlucky. Hardly ever leaves his office, and then when he goes to check the school's still standing, he gets himself gassed.

It's been bad times at school ever since. Three-quarters of the teachers have stopped doing lessons. Mrs Benbarchiche's even been sticking up posters saying 'STOP THE VIOLENCE' and other shock-tactic slogans you'd expect to find in a road safety campaign. It's funny because since the start of the strike she's been hyper-active. It'd be nice if she put as much energy into her lessons as she does into her posters. You never know, maybe she's a militant. A hardliner. A woman with a real political conscience. She might even send off a cheque to Chirac's UMP party from time to time, even if she doesn't look the type with her crow-black hair dye and fuchsia lipstick.

The only teacher not on strike is Mr Lefèvre, the one who talks like that old-skool presenter on the shopping channel. He says the strike's a farce, and the teachers are just layabouts using the attack on Mr Loiseau as an excuse.

I think it's serious, what's happened. I'm not saying Mr Loiseau's the nicest guy in the 93 post-code but still, it shouldn't of turned out like this. Even before he got gassed, it said a lot that Mr Loiseau only felt safe in his office.

Whichever way you look at it, there aren't many students coming out in support of the strike. It's like most of them don't think it'll make any differ-ence and our futures are screwed up anyway.

Last week, Mrs Wotsit came round. That woman's a real shit stirrer. Mum's hardly opened the door when she flashes her perfect white teeth and starts up:

'Dearie me, you're not looking very chirpy today . . . oooh dearie me.'

I bet the reason she's so full of it's because of those twelve free sun-bed sessions she got with her loyalty points at Hey, Good Looking beauty salon. She's coming to the end of the treatment. And another thing, she did a tour of our flat at least ten times like she was visiting the catacombs or something.

'You need to think about changing the washer on that tap.'

She said it with that know-it-all attitude she does way too easily. I'm wondering if she didn't choose this career because dealing with other people's misery cheers her up. Mum went to all the effort of making mint tea for her, but she hardly touched it.

'It's delicious . . .' (she was puckering her lips like a chicken's bum), 'but it *is* . . . er . . . *very sweet* . . . I've got to watch my figure. You know what they say . . . once they're married, women tend to let themselves go.'

She started doing that tinkly giggle, eyes closed and hand to her mouth, Marilyn Monroe style. Who does she think she is? Get with the programme, fool, you've only been married a month.

It didn't bother Mum. She just giggled along with her. Seems like none of this gets to her. I watched her chatting, sitting next to Miss France, and I thought that's how I'd like to be. The woman had criticised Mum's expression, her tap washer, her mint tea, but she didn't care. Just went on giggling and talking with her.

She even told her about the strike and what the situation was at the Formula 1. Then Mrs Thingumyjig suddenly got all serious and suggested Mum did a literacy course at this adult-learning centre in Bondy. She'd learn how to read and write and at the same time she'd get help finding a new job. Mum wouldn't have to pay for any of it. It's covered by the council.

Before she left, she was looking at me and rummaging about in her LOOEY VWEETON bag, and then she went:

'I've got something for you.'

She said it in her high-pitched voice, spelling out each syllable like she's a retard or something. I felt eight months old and like she was telling me she was going to change my nappy now or give me a little pot of artichokes to slurp.

Turns out she gave me a book token so I can get stuff to read for free. I feel like I'm going nowhere with these people treating me like a welfare junkie. BACK RIGHT OFF.

When she closed the door, I thought that was it for the evening, but then the phone rang. It was Aunt Zohra in a panic because the police turned up at hers at six in the morning to arrest Youssef. They broke the door down, kicked him out of bed, trashed the whole flat and took him to the station. Aunt Zohra couldn't stop crying, or not on the telephone at least. She was telling Mum how he's supposed to be mixed up in some story about drug dealing and stolen cars. I think she felt it was her fault because she hadn't looked after her son well enough. By the end, Mum was crying too.

I guess right now Youssef's being interrogated in an airless grey cell. Thing is, I know Youssef, and he's a nice guy. It's not fair. When Mum hung up, we talked a bit, but sometimes words aren't enough. We just stared out of the window, and that said it all. It was grey outside, the same colour as the concrete of the tower blocks and there was a fine drizzle, like God was spitting on us.

I've been having the same dream for a few nights now. One of those crazy dreams you remember perfectly when you wake up, down to the last detail.

I'm opening the window and the sun hits me full in the face. Can't even keep my eyes open. I swing my legs over the windowsill so I'm sitting on the ledge and then, with one push, off I fly. I'm going higher and higher, and the tower blocks are getting smaller and smaller, and look further and further away. I'm flapping my wings, I mean my arms, and then because I'm trying so hard to gain height, I go smack into this wall on my right and get a massive bruise. That's what woke me up, and I'm telling you it's hard coming back to reality with a bump like that.

I told Mrs Burlaud my dream. She kept blinking at me and she said:

'Yes, of course, absolutely . . . It's like the episode with the atlas.'

Come again? Straight up, she calls it an episode. For all I know, Mrs Burlaud isn't a shrink at all. Maybe she works in telly and gets all the material for that sitcom she's writing from the bullshit I'm spinning her. Bet you Burlaud's a pseudonym, her real name's got to be something like Laurence Bouchard. She's part of the script-writing team at AB Productions. That's it . . . Maybe they're already working on the idea. The series'll be a smash hit and get broadcast round the world. Even be dubbed into Japanese. But it's not like I'll see any royalties, I'll just be one of the millions of fans, faceless and fucked over, like all the rest.

Don't know why I even told her about that episode with the atlas. Why do I tell her all the other stuff, for that matter? It was a day when I was bored as a dead rat. I went to the storage cupboard to find the atlas I got for a prize at the end of Year 6.

A storage cupboard's like having an attic, except it's smaller and they're generally in the hallway. It's where you put all the rubbish you never use.

Basically, I opened my atlas at the planisphere, which is where you can fit the whole world in a single page. And seeing how I was having a tough time of it, I drew an escape route on the map.

It was the journey I was going to make one day, through some of the most beautiful places in the world. Yeah OK, so I drew the route in pencil because Mum would of blasted me if she'd seen me doodling in biro all over a new book. But what I'm getting at is I drew up this perfect trip, even if I'm still at the departure point and that departure point is Livry-Gargan.

Any case, I don't know if Mum'd agree to me splitting like that. Wouldn't be anyone around to video *The Young and the Restless* for her. Nobody to go and pick up Sarah from her play-centre either, and Lila'd have all the hassle of finding another babysitter. Makes me realise some people need me, which is good I guess.

Because sometimes, I just want to be someone else, somewhere else, maybe in a whole different time frame. I often picture myself as part of the Ingalls family in *Little House on the Prairie*.

It goes like this: the dad, the mum, the kids, the dog that doesn't bite, the barn and ribbons in your hair for church on Sundays. We're talking happiness, you get me . . . The story's all period atmosphere, like around 1900, with kerosene lamps, the arrival of the railway, prehistoric clothes and other old stuff like that . . . What I like about them is, as soon as something goes wrong, they make the sign of the cross, have a good cry, and everybody's forgotten about it by the next episode ... Just like in the movies.

It's embarrassing because I reckon the characters in that series dress better than me. Even though they live in this tiny arse-end-of-nowhere village and their dad's a fat farmer. Take the hoodie I'm wearing at the moment, not even the Red Cross would want it. Once, I was wearing this mauve sweatshirt with stars on it plus some slogan in English. My mum bought it in a second-hand clothes shop that stank of old stuff. She got them down to one euro for it. She was well chuffed. I didn't want to upset her so I wore it to school but, I don't know, I wasn't feeling it right, I thought there was something odd about that sweatshirt. And sure enough. The fat slags at school, that crew of peroxide blondes with their padded bras and platform heels, never let me hear the end of it. Turns out what was written in English on the sweatshirt meant 'sweet dreams'. That bitch of a mauve sweatshirt was actually a pyjama top. I knew I should of paid more attention to Miss Baker's English lessons in Year 6.

Coming out of school, I ran into Hamoudi. He offered me a ride back home. I was this proud I kind of flaunted it, so all those fruit cakes could see me going off with the spitting image of Antonio Banderas in *Zorro*, except with more scars. But nobody noticed. Too bad.

You know what, at the end of the day, it suits him smelling of cologne and being clean-shaven. You get to see the scar on his chin better. It gives him that 'tormented soul' look, rebel with a heart, that kind of thing . . . Like the hero in some film. The day I asked him how he came by it, he said he couldn't remember. Basically, he didn't want to tell me. Sometimes Hamoudi can be so annoying, when he plays Mystery Man.

I noticed it wasn't the same car as last week. Hamoudi's always changing cars. Either he knows a car dealer who's got a crush on him, or he's dealing in dodgy stuff and I'm not meant to ask questions. That's how it is, between Hamoudi and me. He wants to protect me, doesn't want me getting mixed up in his affairs, so the deal is I hold back on the curiosity.

When I got into the car, I just said hello without looking at him, even though I could see he was staring at me. He didn't start up the engine and I could feel him still looking at me. It was stressing me out.

After a while, he turned my face towards him, smiled at me and said:

'Don't worry! You'll always be my favourite!'

And then he started laughing. Part of me wanted to keep being angry with him, but I couldn't help laughing too because what he said was like a relief. Hamoudi meant that Karine girl I saw him with at the street party with her Frisbee face and high heels. Maybe he thought I was jealous or something . . . You've got to be joking. Any case, it doesn't make sense. She's blonde and wears mauve. Spot the similarity? Me neither.

Actually, it's good for him he's met this girl. At least he's got stuff going on in his life. With me, it's just *kif-kif* tomorrow AKA different day, same shit.

When Hamoudi dropped me off at our block, Aziz from the shop downstairs was waving at me big time. Maybe we need someone else at home. A man who wouldn't clear off to the other side of the Mediterranean or split with a peroxide blonde in high heels. But apart from Aziz, who I reckon's a tiny bit in love with Mum, I don't see who it could be . . .

Aziz is around fifty, I guess. He's short, kind of bald, he's got dirty nails and he's always using the tip of his tongue to try and dislodge what's got stuck between his teeth . . . At the Sidi Mohamed Market, there's a lot of stuff past its sell-by date, plus he charges you more if you take a fizzy drink from the little fridge at the back instead of the front counter. He used to sell bread, until one day a customer found a cock-roach in a baguette and called Environmental Health. On Eid day, Aziz gives Mum a bag full of shopping for free and when we need it, he lets us put things on account, even if we can't always pay him back. Sometimes, he moans on in his accent from the *bled*: 'Oh dirie me! If you iz tiking cridit after cridit, you iz never out of ze woodz!' He's a laugh, Aziz. When you come to pay, he's always got a joke up his sleeve.

'Ze teacher ask Toto: "What it iz twelve bottles of wine, at two euro ze bottle?" And ze little boy he say wot? He say: "Three dayz, Meez . . ."'

And he pisses himself laughing. Aziz may be a con-artist, but he's kind of nice. I reckon lots of people like him around here. At least if Mum married him, we'd never need for anything again.

Yeah, OK, so he's not the boss of some swanky business like Tati but you never know, a few years from now there might be Sidi Mohamed Markets in New York and Moscow.

Mum's finally split from that over-stinky hotel where she got paid twice nothing for flushing the loo after rich gits. Mr Schmidt didn't even give her the leaving pay she was owed, made out it was because of the strike and all that . . . I know it's illegal. Any case, without Mum, Mr Schmidt's motel's heading straight for bankruptcy. She's got this special technique for making beds, kind of gentle but strong at the same time, so there isn't a single wrinkle on the sheet, better than in the army. Personally, I'm glad she's not working at the Formula 1 in Bagnolet any more. What's there to miss? Not the hours or the pay or that rat-head of a boss Mr Schmidt.

It's actually thanks to Livry-Gargan town council. I say 'actually' because it's not easy to admit that Barbie doll social worker Mrs Wotsit helped Mum find her 'dual training course'. 'Dual' means you're juggling two different things. Like when you mix sweet and sour, or husband and lover. Mum's going to do Literacy.

They're going to teach her to read and write in the language of my country. With a teacher, a blackboard, exercise books with big lines, and she'll even get homework too. I'll help her with it, if she wants.

I'm thinking neeky Nabil comes in handy when I'm totally lost in chemistry and he explains all those exercises Mrs Benbarchiche's set us. This time it's the isotopes. But with her Tunisian accent, it comes out sounding like 'ZZ Top's, and I'm picturing that rock group of ageing beards in sunglasses . . .

It's funny, Mum's totally dreading this course. She never went to school, so she's flipping out. Getting up at five o'clock in the morning to work in some cheapskates' motel and wreck her health, no problem. But now it's for real. She's going to learn about job-seeking techniques as well. That way, I'm hoping she'll find something *nice*. She'll get paid while she's on the course and she doesn't finish late, gets off practically the same time as me. So I'll see lots more of her, and I won't keep forgetting I've got a mum.

She's starting in two weeks and it's like safe because between now and then, when I come home from school at midday, there'll be something else to eat apart from tinned tuna.

*　　*　　*

What Mum really likes watching on telly in the evenings is the weather forecast. Specially when it's that presenter with brown hair, the one who tried out for the musical *The Birdcage* but didn't get it because he was over the top ... So there he was, talking about this huge cyclone in the Caribbean, and it was like oh my days, this crazy thing getting ready to do loads of damage. Franky, this hurricane was called. Mum said she thought the western obsession with giving names to natural disasters was totally stupid. I like it when Mum and me get a chance to have deep and meaningful conversations.

Aziz is friendly, but you've got a one in three chance of landing on stuff past its sell-by date at his shop, so sometimes I go to Malistar, a tiny mini-market that's been around for years even if it's changed its name loads of times. We're talking at least ten reincarnations since I've been here: World Provisions, Better Price, Allprice ... Trouble is, everyone calls this shop something different, depending on which name stuck with them.

So anyway, I went to Malistar to buy some sanitary towels, the no-brand kind, with fluorescent orange packaging like the jackets lollipop ladies wear when they're helping kids cross the road. Even just the packaging is like big shame. You can't hide away in that shop and afterwards, on the estate, everyone knows you've got your period. When I get to the till, big suprise, the queue's from Paris to Dakar. Except, instead of the car rally, you're on a bike it's going that slowly ... When it finally gets to my turn, another stroke of luck: the packet won't go through the till. It was making this noise like a scratched 45 each time the cashier tried swiping it. The cashier's called Monique and one thing's for sure, she's got the right face for the job. She's so flat you could fax her. Plus, if I was her, I'd sue the hairdresser who gave her that mullet. Monique must get her sense of humour from the sketch shows she watches on video, Sunday afternoons. So anyway, seeing as Monique still couldn't swipe the flipping packet of sanitary towels and she'd had enough, instead of typing in the bar code like they do at ATAC supermarket, she grabbed the microphone to make an announcement. That's when my legs started shaking and I had these beads of sweat sliding down my face like bomb disposal experts before they cut the red wire. So she yells in that deep voice of hers – she didn't realise there's no point shouting seeing as that's what mikes are for:

'RAYMOND!!! How much is the *24 + get 2 free* pack of sanitary towels, regular with padding and wings?!'

She waits a second and then starts up again:

'Yoo-hoo! Raymond!! You asleep or what?'

Then we heard this diabolical voice roaring that the bloody packet was two euros thirty-eight.

The most embarrassing thing of all is I didn't even have enough to pay her and she had to put it on account for me. If I'd known, I wouldn't of had my period . . .

When I got back home, Mum was on the phone to Aunt Zohra again. Youssef's case is coming to court soon, that's why Aunt Zohra's so worried. She keeps calling Mum, even late at night because she's having trouble sleeping. They have these long conversations together, with lots of heavy silences. I know because Mum sticks the phone on loudspeaker.

'I'm telling you Yasmina, my sister, you're lucky you never had a son, God is with you, you just don't realise . . .'

' . . .'

'I mean, it's easier with a daughter! You know something, I'd never seen my son cry . . . Yesterday, when I went to visit him, he wept in my arms, like a woman, it breaks my heart . . .'

'May God come to your help!'

'May he hear you, my sister . . . What am I going to say to my man when he gets back from the *bled*? He'll be here in two months . . .'

'Ask God for your son back . . .'

Seems like the two of them are counting a lot on God. I hope Youssef gets off quickly. He doesn't deserve all this stupid stuff happening to him. I can't say I know much about the legal system. All I've got to go on are old *Perry Mason* episodes. In one of them there was this judge who nodded off during the trial but that didn't stop people calling him 'Your Honour'.

I just don't get what's fair about justice if Youssef goes to prison.

He's going down. He got a year. Aunt Zohra's disgusted with life. She's mostly scared about what happens when that crazy old husband of hers gets back next month. Reda and Hamza, her two other sons, are in free-fall at school and they're always getting into fights with other guys on their estate because of being called 'bastard' seeing as their dad's hardly ever there. As for Youssef, it's the Grey Bar Hotel for him, and even if he was always joking me, it's not like he deserved to lose a year of his life in such a stupid way.

It's like Hamoudi. After prison, he did loads of part-time work and shitty odd jobs that all turned out a nightmare. He's never really got it together since. These days, he lives off dealing and can't lead a normal life. It's not like they've come up with a pension scheme, or a special social security benefit for dealers yet. Any case, I'd never imagined it happening to Youssef. If a clairvoyant had told me that a few months ago, I wouldn't of believed her.

* * *

My mum told me how back in the home country, when she was still living with her folks, her aunt and this woman who was their neighbour took her to see a clairvoyant. Everyone was worried about Mum refusing to get married. The clairvoyant told her the man she was destined to marry would come from the other side of the sea to find her and that he worked with earth and stone. It ended up being my dad. It's true: he came to find her from the other side of the sea, from France; and by boat, because it was cheaper than the plane. And it's true about the earth and stone bit seeing as how, at the time, he was working for Public Building Works. But the clairvoyant forgot to mention how it would all turn out. People like that only say what you want to hear.

That's how it was with Sherif. Sherif's this guy from the estate who turned up from Tunisia about six years ago. He's tagged Sherif because he's got a real cowboy look about him. Plus he always wears a red cap with a star printed on it. His black hair and moustache make him look like he's just walked out of a Western. So this guy goes to see a clairvoyant who tells him he'll get very rich soon. It's been this many years since she told him that. Maybe she should of been more specific about what she meant by 'soon'. So basically, every day since then, Sherif puts money on the horses, and totally believes in it. He goes to the newsagent's in the square to get the results. And seeing how he loses every time, he gets jittery. Sherif's a Mediterranean guy, you get me ... When he doesn't win, meaning always, he crumples his cap, shouts all these insults in Arabic and leaves. This has been going on for a while.

Sometimes, I think about how life's a stroke of luck all the same. We make out it's not a bowl of roses, but what about those people who are even worse off ... Yeah, they do exist, believe me. Like that boy at my primary school who was always getting beaten up. Small blond kid with glasses. He had a season ticket for the front row in class, always got top marks, used to give the teacher pancakes on Shrove Tuesday and ate pork in the school canteen. Your dream victim.

Mum's started her new training course. She likes it a lot, from what she's telling me. She's even found two other women she gets on with: a Moroccan from Tangier and a granny from Normandy called 'Jiklin'. I'm guessing this trainer's called Jacqueline. Makes me realise my mum's sociable, not like me. When I was little and Mum used to take me to the sandpit, none of the other kids wanted to play with me. I called it 'the French kids' sandpit' because it was bang in the middle of an estate with houses instead of tower blocks and they're mostly white French families. One time, they were all making a circle and wouldn't hold my hand because it was the day after the Eid, the festival of the Sheep, and Mum had put some henna on the palm of my right hand. They were asking for a slapping, those morons: thought I was dirty.

Talk about no clue when it comes to diversity and melting pots. Then again, I guess it's not really their fault. There's a big fat divide between the Paradise estate where I live and the houses on the Rousseau estate. We're talking massive wire fencing that stinks of rust it's so old, plus a stone wall that runs the whole length. It's worse than the Maginot Line or the Berlin Wall. On our side, there's a loads of tags, spray paintings and posters for concerts and different North African evenings, plus graffiti giving it up for Saddam Hussein or Che Guevara, patriotic signs, '*Viva Tunisia*', '*Stand Up Senegal*', even rap lyrics with a philosophical slant. But what I like best on the wall is an old drawing that's been there since back in the day, long before the rise of rap or the start of the war in Iraq. It's an angel in handcuffs with a red cross over its mouth.

There's a girl being held prisoner on the eleventh floor of my block. She's called Samra and she's nineteen. Her brother follows her everywhere. He stops her going out and when she gets back from school a bit later than normal, he grabs her by the hair and the dad finishes off the job. Once, I even heard Samra screaming because they'd locked her in. In their family, the men are kings. They've got Samra under close surveillance and her mum can't do anything, can't say anything either. Anyone'd think it was bad luck to be a girl, or something.

But a few days ago, some neighbours told Mum Samra had run away. For the last three weeks everyone's been looking for her. Her dad's even got the police involved. They've stuck up posters all over, in the shops, post office, tower block lobbies, schools . . . The photo's from when Samra was in Year 6. Her brace didn't come out so well in the photocopy.

Makes me think of that TV programme *Out*

of Sight, the one where they traced people. There were guys who hadn't seen members of their family for over twenty years. It was too much, this show. They even managed to find them when they'd changed their face, name, everything. It worked every time, apart from when they were dead. Afterwards, when they did the reunion bit, people were blubbing and fainting. It turned into a spectacle. One time, they found this cousin in Sidney, Australia. They filmed his place, his new family, new job and all that. But I thought it was tough on the guy who'd been cut up about the disappearance all those years, who'd bust a gut to find his cousin only to realise he didn't give a shit and had a great new life thanks very much.

So anyway, right now in the neighbourhood, everybody's talking about Samra disappearing. They're even saying people have seen her in Paris with a big tummy. Meaning she's pregnant . . . The rumour goes from Aziz's shop to the school gates via the dry cleaner's. When Samra was locked up at home in her concrete cage, nobody talked about it, like they found it completely normal. Now that she's managed to break free from that dictator of a brother and her torturer dad, people are accusing her. I don't get it.

*   *   *

Take Youseff, now he *can't* escape. Aunt Zohra called us again to tell us about her last visit. She keeps saying how he's losing weight and his eyes are blank. She doesn't recognise her son any more and I think it really scares her. Still, it seems to me like she's getting braver. She's coping better than at the beginning. She just needed time to get used to it, that's all. It's horrible to think how suffering can make you get used to anything, specially the worst.

Youssef's dad is coming back in two weeks and I'm wondering what's going to happen. Mum's helping Aunt Zohra get tactical. She says it's all about how you say these things. For bad news, you've got to look to the telly. Like Gaby's courage and tact in *Sunset Beach* when she tells her fool of a husband that she cheated on him with his own brother. Oh and he was a priest, by the way, the brother. So it's like even worse. Compared to that, telling Youssef's dad his kid's in prison till next spring is a piece of cake. Like me telling Mum I've got to stay down a year at school. First of all, I'll have to explain what staying down a year means, seeing as she hasn't got a clue when it comes to the French educational system. Then I'll need to follow it up by saying it's so I'm more successful in the long run. For her, success means working in an office with a swivel chair on wheels, a telephone and a radiator not far from the swivel chair on wheels.

The other evening, I hung around on the landing for a bit, discussing stuff with Hamoudi. We were talking about parents and the teenage phase because Mrs Burlaud had explained to me what that meant.

Hamoudi thinks it's just an excuse, made up by Western parents who messed up raising their kids properly. I don't agree. He can be hardcore sometimes, Hamoudi. He told me he wouldn't even of begun to think about throwing a teenage fit because his dad would of known how to sort him out, straight up. And another thing, he told me it's over with Karine, the dumb blonde I met at the summer festival. When he said that, his voice sounded a bit sad. I know it's not right, but deep down I felt glad. I was thinking how Hamoudi and me'd get back to where we were before. To cheer him up I told him, any days, she had a face like a Frisbee. That cracked him up. He didn't tell me why they split up, though. But I don't reckon she cheated on him with Hamoudi's brother who's not a priest.

He didn't tell me because he thinks it's for grown-ups and none of my business. He's not completely wrong.

That fat dumpling, AKA neeky Nabil, came round to help me with my Citizenship Studies homework the other night. The essay title sounded like one of those current affairs programmes on TV: 'Why Don't People Vote?'

Me and neeky Nabil talked about it. To give you an example, he thinks a guy from the Paradise estate who left school back in the day, can't get a job, parents not working, shares a bedroom with his four younger brothers: 'Why'd he give a shit about voting?' Nabil's right. The guy's got to fight just to survive each day, so you can forget about being a good citizen . . . If things worked out better for him, maybe he'd shift his arse and vote. Except I don't really see who'd represent him. Well that's it, isn't it: *he's* the guy you should be asking 'Why Don't People Vote?' Not a class of pizza-faced fifteen-year-olds.

Maybe that's why so many estates are mashed up: not enough of the people on them vote. You're not useful, politically speaking, if you don't vote. When I'm eighteen, I'll vote. You never get a chance to speak out round here. So when you've got it, grab it.

Anyway, that evening, instead of leaving when we'd done and going back home to his mum, Nabil just stayed there, talking, and finishing off the packet of crackers on the table. I thought they'd last the week, my crackers, but too bad I guess. When Mr Neek finally decided to jet, I saw him to the front door, and the look on his face suddenly changed. He came over all serious, moved up close and personal and kissed me on the lips. For real.

How dare him! He doesn't just stuff his face with all my crackers, but then he goes and kisses me without asking. The worst is, like a mule-head, I couldn't think of anything to say. I just went as red as the peppers my mum stews up and shut the door mumbling 'bye' so quietly he probably never even heard. Then I ran to drink a long glass of mint cordial and brushed my teeth, twice, to get rid of the taste of Nabil.

So what do I do now? I could try telling people I fell off my bike, blacked out, woke up with amnesia and don't remember a thing, as in zilch, zip, nada . . . Trouble is, nobody'll believe me. Everyone knows I haven't got a bike and can't afford one either. Plan B: have plastic surgery and turn into someone else so he can't recognise me and never tries gluing his disgusting chapped lips to mine again. YUK!

It wasn't exactly how I'd imagined my first kiss. No, I was picturing more of a dream setting, you get me, at the edge of a lake, in a forest, at sunset, with a buff guy who'd look a bit like Thierry Henry in the Renault ads, when he's doing that *Va-va-voom* line and the camera closes in on his toothpaste smile ... Anyway, the guy would be explaining how you can start a fire with a nail file and stone, when we'd break out of our deep and meaningful conversation to turn gently towards each other, and we'd kiss like it was the most natural thing in the world, like we'd been doing it all our lives. Of course, when I picture that scene, my hair's all slick, I'm looking sharp and my boobs are bigger.

The story of Nabil's mouth is *not* going to get out. Talk about die of shame. Not even Mrs Burlaud knows, and especially not Mum. If she finds out, she'll kill me. I'm mad at Nabil for stealing my first kiss, and cleaning out my packet of crackers, but not as mad as I thought I'd be. Well, *I* know what I mean.

Round at Mrs Burlaud's on Monday, we did something new, kind of like a game. She was showing me these big-format photos, flipping through them quickly and I had to say 'like it' or 'don't like it'.

Most of the time I said whatever because she was going so fast and there was no time to think. So for example, I said 'don't like it' to the photo of a small baby. And big surprise, Mrs Burlaud stopped on that photo. She started talking about my so-called half-brother, like I hadn't seen *that* coming. She was making out that's why, subconsciously you get me, I said 'don't like it'. Mum and me know it's a boy now. A neighbour from Morocco sent us a letter. It was in French, just to make it even more humiliating for her. I had to read it out.

Seriously though, what's the point in over-complicating stuff? No connection, I told Mrs Burlaud. She was going too fast and I hadn't seen the photo properly. I made a mistake, that's all. I mean, come off it. You don't have to like babies. Babies cry all the time, they stink and dribble and poo in their nappies. Plus the baby in the photo was this ugly, like a chunky croissant.

And another thing, that other brat isn't my brother. He just happens to be the son of my *how-big-is-my-beard* dad. It's not the same. I'm telling you, Mrs Burlaud's bare stupid when she makes out she's got an answer for everything and has that smug grin on her face like Harrison Ford at the end of *Indiana Jones*. Right now, she keeps banging on about how I'm growing and it's normal to question stuff. Growing? Man, it's time she changed her specs! I've been one metre sixty a while now and nothing's happening. Or maybe she meant like I'm growing up. Yeah, must of been that.

Lila makes these marks in black pencil on Sarah's bedroom door and writes the date next to them, to measure how tall she is. It's fun having this little trail of marks, one above the other. When she grows up, she'll get a kick out of seeing it again. And another thing, round at Sarah's, there are loads of photos from when she was a tiny baby right up to now.

She's lucky. I haven't got any photos of me

before I was three. After that, they're school photos . . . It makes me sad when I think about it. As if I don't totally exist. Bet if I'd got a willy, I'd have a big fat pile of photo albums.

One day, coming back from the play-scheme with Sarah, we dropped by on Hamoudi.

'So you're Sarah are you, princess?'

'Yes.'

'You're pretty cute in that pink dress, just like a fairy.'

'Dew-no-wot, you've got NOT NICE teeth, you should ask the tooth fairy to look after you . . .'

I gave Sarah a bit of a telling off. Told her it wasn't polite to say things like that. But Hamoudi couldn't of cared less. In fact, he roared with laughter. Well, you've got to admit Hamoudi's teeth are kind of lousy. But it's not like they're a disaster zone either. Only what you'd expect, after all he's smoked over the years.

So anyway, he's been crazy about Sarah ever since. Tells me there's nothing more refreshing than kids because they're genuine, spontaneous, for real, you get me. 'They're the only honest thing left in our corrupt and hypocritical society.' Maybe Hamoudi's right. He's doing a lot of thinking these days. And he's looking for a job. Or that's what he told me. He needs to go straight for a while, what with dealing getting risky. Plus, like he says, 'I'm not seventeen any more . . .' I could see the regret in his eyes. 'I'm nearly a third of the way through my life, and I've done nothing. Sweet FA.' I told him it wasn't too late and if he was talking like that, maybe it was because he was scared of changing things. Don't know where I got that from. Must be from watching daytime chat shows: 'He cheated on me and yes it's my business.' Still, it's strange Hamoudi's thinking like this because there's always been a lot of freedom in his family, he could do whatever he wanted. Only one thing he couldn't do: cry. Because he's a man and Hamoudi's dad says men don't cry. Maybe that played a part. People don't realise how important it is to cry.

It's the summer holidays already. I saw the Ali family set off for Morocco this afternoon. They've got this big red van and every year they drive down through France and Spain to spend two months in the *bled*. I was watching them from my window. They took at least an hour to load up. The kids were all sharply dressed. You could see from their faces how happy and excited they were to be heading off. It made me feel jealous. Whatever, they were taking tons of luggage. Three-quarters of those bags must of been full of presents for family, friends and neighbours. It's always like that. Mum Ali was even taking a vacuum cleaner. Rowenta, latest model. She'll get respect with that, over there.

Plus they'll get to see their new house all finished. If you ask me, they got it built by eating rice and pasta every meal so they could send money to the builders back in the *bled*. And if the mum's taking a vacuum cleaner it means they're planning on settling down there. I bet that hasn't crossed the kids' minds. But I reckon the parents have been thinking about it ever since they first came to France. Ever since they made the mistake of setting foot in this bloody country they thought they'd be able to call their own.

Some people spend their whole lives hoping they'll make it back home. But a lot only go back once, in a coffin, dispatched by plane like they're cargo or something. They reach home soil again all right, but not quite the way they were expecting to.

Then again, some of them do manage to get back. Like the one who used to play at being my dad. Except he left without any luggage.

Sometimes, I try imagining what I'd be like if my parents were Polish or Russian instead of Moroccan. Maybe I'd be an ice-dancing champion, but not in those cheapskate local competitions where you win chocolate medals and T-shirts. No, I'm talking real skating, like in the Olympic Games, with fancy classical music, guys who've flown in from around the world to mark your performance, like at school, and whole stadiums to cheer you even if you go splat like a steak. Whatever, the important thing's to do it with style. Oh my days, skating is too much, and those dresses, man, with loads of sequins, and netting and colours and stuff. Trouble is, those outfits mean you can always see the girls' knickers. So my mum wouldn't be too happy if I was ice-dancing on telly. And another thing, if I was Russian, my name would be totally unpronounce-able and chances are I'd be blonde. Shitty prejudices, I know. There must be Russian brunettes out there with easy-peasy names to say, so easy you'd call out to them just for the kick of saying such a no-problem name. Plus, for all I know, maybe there's some Russian girls who never tried on a pair of skates in their life.

So basically everybody's jetting off, and I'm staying in the ends, keeping an eye on the estate like a guard dog and waiting for the others to come back all tanned from their holidays. Even Nabil's disappeared. Maybe he's gone back to Tunisia with his parents.

Any case, seeing how school's over, he won't be coming round to help me with my home-work or rewrite my essays any more. Actually, I'm done with essays for ever, apart from if we get assignments on blow-drying and hair curlers. Oh yes, I forgot to tell you: I can't repeat the year because there aren't enough places for everybody at school. And that 'everybody' includes me. So they found me a place last minute at this college not so far from home, doing hairdressing. Hamoudi was this angry when I told him. Said he was going to pay them a visit, give them what for, contact the local education authority, get on the council's case, stuff like that ... Said they've got no right to decide for me. I told him I didn't know what I should be doing anyway, seeing as nobody's ever given me any careers advice. Plus, who knows, I might really enjoy hairdressing. Yeah, come to think of it, I'm going to get a kick out of doing perms on old bags who spend a fortune on their hair even when they've only got three whiskers on their skull.

There's this girl on the estate who studied hairdressing. She hasn't got enough money to open a salon but she still wants to be her own boss, so she cuts people's hair in their own homes. It's doing well. When there's a wedding in the neighbourhood, everyone calls her up. The girls ask for a blow-dry and get her to pull really hard with the brush to make like their hair's naturally straight. But they start sweating after a couple of dances, and all it takes is a few curly wisps to give the game away.

Talking about weddings, there's one happening here soon, and it's Aziz, the famous proprietor of the Sidi Mohamed Market, the meanest shopkeeper on earth. I'm kind of pissed off he's getting married because that means it's all over for Mum . . .

Rachida, who's our neighbour and the biggest gossip I know, told us Aziz is marrying a girl from Morocco. I'm starting to see why there are so many single women round here. If men think they can go into import-export . . . It's a shame our weddings aren't like in the States where the priest says that famous line: *'If any person knows why they may not be joined together, let them speak now or forever hold their peace.'* At this point, there's always some Mr Braveheart who dares interrupt the ceremony because he's been secretly in love with the bride for eight years. He tells her this, and she says she feels the same way, with tears in her eyes. The husband's a good loser – even if he's kind of fuming – and shakes Braveheart's hand: 'No hard feelings, old chap!' Then he lends him the tux he's paid a fortune to hire for the day and Braveheart gets to marry the girl instead of the good-loser groom.

Mum could do the same thing for Aziz's wedding. Tell Aziz he's the most romantic guy in the neighbourhood and that she's had strong feelings for him for years even though he's bald and has filthy nails . . . I've got to stop thinking in films. I know she'd never do it. Plus there'll be the whole estate at Aziz's wedding, and if Mum did that, it'd be big shame. We call it 'hchouma'. Anyway, we don't even know if he's inviting us. He's given us so much credit we've never paid back. Whatever, nobody ever invites us anywhere. Way after the party's over, people come round to see Mum and say sorry they forgot about her. It doesn't matter. Mum and me couldn't care less about not being part of the jet set.

Sunday morning, Mum and me went to this car boot sale. She was looking for a pair of shoes because she's got a small hole on her left shoe, and when it rains or she walks on the grass in the morning her toes get soaked.

We were walking between the pitches when I heard these girls behind us:

'Check out the daughter, her garm's even worse than her old lady's. It's like she's straight out of the car boot too!'

'Yeah, whatever, car boot's like department store shopping for them.'

They were wetting themselves. Sniggering into their hands. I looked at Mum but it didn't seem like she'd heard anything. She was staring at this single sleeve for some old crooner. In the photo, he had big hair, you get me. It's like they repatriated all the hairdressers in the eighties, hid them in a cave, and they only started showing up again at the beginning of the nineties.

So, to cut a long story short, I didn't even turn

round to eat them alive, those two slags behind us. I didn't rip out their nostrils or anything. I just made like nothing had happened, like I hadn't heard. I held Mum's arm and squeezed it hard because I was pumped full of rage and then the tears were welling up in my eyes and my nose was stinging. I badly wanted to cry, but I really tried to hold it together. I made myself because I didn't want to tell Mum about it. She'd of felt guilty. And anyway, she was checking out these potato-peelers at one euro the bundle, so I didn't want to disturb her. Times like that, I wish I was stronger with a protective shell to keep me safe for the rest of my life. So nothing could ever get under my skin.

The whole estate went to Aziz's wedding. They held it in this big hall in Livry-Gargan with a real orchestra over specially from Fès. Aziz hired two 'négafas', who are like women matchmakers responsible for organising the party: decorations, clothes, make-up, the bride's jewellery, food, that kind of stuff. It was a big fat wedding. Aziz splashed out bare dough. Or that's what I heard because, you guessed it – we weren't invited.

We don't see Mrs Thingumyjig, the social worker from the council any more because she's off on maternity leave. Said she'd be back after her baby's born. It annoyed me when she said that. Sounded like: 'You'll still be poor in a year's time, you'll still need me.' And another thing, while we're waiting for her to come back, we're stuck with this dodgy replacement who's always got her eyes half-shut behind these massive bottle-lens glasses with chunky pink frames. Plus she talks *very slowly* in this horror-film voice, the kind you can imagine saying: 'I am Death! Follow me, your turn has come!' Still, I'm not so bothered by that stuff. Don't give a shit, to be honest. My beef is, she makes me feel as if Mum and me are just numbers in her file. Does her job like she's on automatic. Like she's a robot programmed for it. Bet if you scratched the skin on her back, dug right into her flesh, you'd find an aluminium coating underneath, a few screws and a serial number. I'm calling her Cyborg Services.

I'm not looking after Sarah this week because her mum's got holiday leave and both of them are off to Lila's sister in Toulouse. It's hard being separated from people that matter to you.

I'm thinking of Aunt Zohra and Youssef and some others too . . .

Talking of Aunt Zohra, she plucked up the courage to tell her old crazy all about it. Things got violent between them and the old nutter started hitting Aunt Zohra. After a while he had to lay off because his arms hurt too much and he'd got palpitations. So he sat down and asked her for a glass of water. She went to get him one and that was the end of it.

She told us everything. Every day, she asks God for him to go back to the *bled*. When I think how, not so long ago, Mum was praying for ours to come back . . .

She's not so lost in her thoughts these days. And she's looking better. She's able to read a few words and she's very proud she can write her first name without any mistakes. At first, she used to write S backwards, like babies do. Yeah OK, so I can see she's still anxious sometimes, like when she's watching the telly and it's switched off. But it doesn't happen so often. Plus she's active and free which was no way the case before. When Dad lived with us, there was no question of her working even though it was a nightmare us being skint. According to Dad, women weren't made for working.

By the way, yesterday Hamoudi told me he'd found a job. He stumbled on the ad in that free paper, *Paris Boum Boum*. This hire firm for hi-fi, video and computer equipment was looking for someone to do security. He called up straight away, got an interview and, bam, they took him on. He says it's kind of a pain because it's night work, but he's happy he's found a proper job, says it's better that way. OK so it feels like they hired him to be their guard dog, but he doesn't give a shit.

Makes me think of some of those houses on the Rousseau estate. They've got signs up with a photo of a massive Doberman who's bare scary and a 'Beware of the dog!' speech bubble, even though everyone knows what's in that house is a toy poodle called Grandpa who's scared stiff of kids and flies.

Monday, round at Mrs Burlaud's, things were *different*. To start with, when I got there, she told me to make myself comfortable and then she left the room saying: 'I'll be right back!' like the commercial breaks in one of those variety shows on telly. Only she didn't come back for twenty minutes, and when she did I noticed she smelled of alcohol. Like smelled *a lot*. But that was nothing compared to ... I didn't have much to say that session so, at one point, she crossed her short little legs and went: 'Perhaps you've got a funny story to tell me?' That was when I noticed she was wearing suspenders. I looked at her face then down at her suspenders and back again and thought, well, that's not a bad joke for starters. Then she was asking me loads of questions about Mum, nosey stuff about her personal life and everything. I told her she didn't have one any more since HE left. Mrs Burlaud wanted to know if I could see Mum making a new life for herself with another man. Can I see it? I'm planning it, aren't I?

*   *   *

I watched a programme about being single and new ways to meet people. There are these things called 'speed dates'. As in, getting it together fast. I know this because at 'Speed Burger' you order your hamburger and it's ready in two minutes flat. Plus it's 100 per cent halal. Basically, these speed dates are like organised meeting places. You sit opposite somebody you don't know for seven minutes. Long enough to say: 'I don't like your face' or 'D'you still live with your mum?' Except I can't really see Mum in a place like that. It's not like I actually believe she'll get it together with someone else. I was just saying it because I'd like her to, that's all.

The only way would be if they came directly round to the house and asked for her hand in marriage. Trouble is, she's hardly ever here now, apart from this month because her course stops during the holidays. I'm going to stick up a timetable on the door for when she's here, like at the doctors', with some of our selection requirements.

Alcoholics, old men, cowards need not apply.
Thank you in advance.

Preferably: Hard worker, cultivated, witty, charming, good teeth, stamp collector, likes tinned tomatoes.

Yeah, OK, so I was a bit harsh about the old men, but definitely no alcoholics. I don't ever again want to stand outside Bar Constantine in town, waiting for him to finish knocking it back so I can take him home because he doesn't remember the way when he's drunk. Or prostitute my pride at the Sidi Mohamed Market buying bumper packs of beer during Ramadan and then lugging the empty bottles down to the recyling bins afterwards. It made such a noise when the bottles smashed inside the bins, everybody in our block knew how much Dad had necked. All that recycled glass could of won him a civic medal, or made him a mascot for the Green party. I'd of given anything to swap Dad for Joe McGann in *The Upper Hand*, but he was already taken. Now it's definitely not going to happen.

Hamoudi really liked that job. He was getting used to the idea of going straight. But they fired him because things went missing from the warehouse. At least six thousand euros' worth of gear and Hamoudi got the blame. Not even his parents believed him when he denied it. Any case, they're convinced he's good for nothing, and they keep telling him so.

At least I believed him. 'I don't care, I'm clean, I've got nothing to blame myself for, I did a good job and I never fell asleep. Only thing they can hold against me is this filthy face . . .' He was pointing to himself as he said it, eyes wide open. I didn't dare tell him he was handsome. Scared he'd get the wrong idea. Hamoudi's got dark brown hair, a great olive complexion and big hazel eyes . . . Mediterranean looks, you get me. Says that's why they unfairly accused him. Perhaps he's paranoid, but they had no right to accuse him without proof. That's out of order.

*   *   *

Life's full of disappointments. On my way back from the market this morning, I overheard two girls and some guy talking on the bus. The girls were twins, or nearly. Same clothes, same hair, they even talked the same.

The guy was short and had his mouth open all the time. On the plus side, he didn't say anything, thank God. Just listened. The girls were chewing gum and blowing bubbles at the end of nearly every sentence.

'You know *The Pretender*?'

'Yeah, heavy!' (Bubble.)

'D'you watch it every day?' (Bubble.)

'Yeah!'

'You know the main character?'

'Heavy!' (Bubble.)

'He's called Jarod.' (Bubble.)

'Yeah, heavy! He's buff, man!

'Well he's gay!' (Bubble.)

'For real?'

'Gay, for real.' (Bubble.)

'Oh my days! How d'you know?' (Bubble.)

'It's my sister, innit, she saw it on the Internet.'

'Issit? Oh my days! Like gay, for real, on the Internet . . .' (Bubble.)

Not Jarod. You could of said James Dean to me, or Michael Jackson, OK. But not Jarod. I could never follow the story in that series: he was the only reason I stayed crouched in front of the telly like a mule-head. He's drop-dead gorgeous. Gay men don't know how lucky they are.

Mrs Burlaud's always saying I'll be disappointed by stuff my whole life and I've just got to get used to it. Yeah but not this. This wasn't written in my contract.

It's weird, but I can't stop thinking about neeky Nabil. Still can't work out why he suddenly decided to glue his fat mouth to mine. And another thing, he's got massive lips. I was scared he'd inhale me and I'd be a prisoner inside him. Once I got out again, all the TV channels in the world would film me talking about my stay inside neeky Nabil. And then I'd write a book called *Voyage Inside Nabil*. Bet you it'd be a bestseller.

It'd be good to find out when he's coming back, just so I know. Oh yeah, and to tell him he's got some explaining to do: on top of his acne, he bugs the shit out of everyone.

Seeing as Mum's still on holiday till next week, we decided to wander round Paris together. It was the first time she'd seen the Eiffel Tower for real, even though she's been living half an hour from it for almost twenty years. Before now, it was just something on the TV news on New Year's Eve, when it's all lit up and underneath it people are partying, dancing, kissing and getting wasted. Whatever, she was bare impressed.

'It must be two or three times our block, isn't it?'

Straight up, I told her. Except our block and the estates round here generally don't get so much tourist interest. It's not like you find camera-toting Japanese mafia standing at the bottom of the tower blocks in this neighbourhood. The only interested ones are journalists and they just spin big fat lies with their sick reports about violence in the suburbs.

Mum would of happily spent hours looking at it. Personally, I think it's ugly, but you can't deny it's there. The Eiffel Tower is like this big statement. I'd like to of gone up in the red and yellow lifts, ketchup-mayo style, but it was too expensive. And another thing, we'd of had to queue up behind the Germans, the Italians, the English and loads of other tourists who aren't scared of heights or spending their cash. We didn't have enough money to buy a miniature Eiffel Tower either. They're even uglier than the original but still, it's classy to have one on your telly. Tourist-trap stalls are so expensive. Plus what those guys sell is like total crap. After that, this pigeon shat on my shoulder. I tried wiping myself against a statue of Gustave Eiffel 1832–1923, but the bird shit had gone hard and wouldn't shift. In the RER train, people were staring at the mark and I felt *hchouma*. I was this fed up because it's the only jacket I have that doesn't make me look poor. If I wear any of the others, everybody calls me 'Cosette' from *Les Misérables*. Anyway, who cares, whether it shows or not I'll still be poor. Later, when my boobs are bigger and I'm a bit cleverer, when I'm a grown-up you get me, I'll join an outfit that helps people . . .

It does my head in knowing there are people who need you and you can be useful to them.

One of these days, if I don't need my blood or one of my kidneys, I could donate them to sick people who've had their name on the list for the longest time. But I wouldn't just do it for a clear conscience, so I could look myself in the eye when I was taking off my make-up after work, but because I really wanted to.

Lila and Sarah are back from Toulouse, and they brought me some cakes. Probably got nothing to do with Toulouse, those cakes, but it was a nice gesture I thought. Lila told me about their time down there at her sister's. And then she talked a lot about herself, and what her life was like before coming to the Paradise estate, with Sarah's dad and everything . . .

Lila's from Algeria originally, like Aunt Zohra. She left her family early on to live the way she wanted, like in the novels she was reading at sixteen. Her and Sarah's dad met very young, fell in love straight away. Their story began like in those Sunday matinées, with never-ending walks on beautiful July days and 'I love you' every ten metres.

Trouble was, both families were against it. Sarah's dad's family are from Brittany and they go back at least, I don't know, eighteen generations, while with Lila, it's more like the traditional Algerian family worried about preserving religion and traditions. So they were all worked up about it from the start, plus her ex-husband's family aren't so good with suntans. They decided to get married anyway, even though they were already pulling apart as a couple. Looking back on it, Lila says she realises they did it more out of rebellion than love. Her wedding day is one hell of a bad memory. Atmosphere like death, hardly any guests on her side, and, surprise surprise, loads of pork in the meal cooked by her father-in-law. It was touch and go if he'd put it in the wedding cake too, just for kicks. What really made him laugh was dropping clangers about religion. Bang on quarter to eight, every family meal – at least the ones she was invited to – out came the atheist joke. Even though Lila was already feeling uncomfortable enough as it was.

And then one day she'd had enough, of her father-in-law's jokes, of salami with the apéritifs, of her long-term unemployed husband slumped on the settee goggling at repeats on the TV and drinking beer with a name that's a date from the middle of the seventeenth century. So she asked for a divorce and since then it hasn't been easy. These days, she's bringing up her little girl all by herself, but she's still hoping to meet her 'perfect match'. It made me think of an article about single mums I read in a magazine lying about on the coffee table in the doctors' waiting room. Main thing is, I've understood why, behind the supermarket cashier who cuts out fashionable articles from *Woman Today*, Lila's a big dreamer.

You never know, maybe there's something in what women's magazines say about the perfect man, after all. They have these three-page articles explaining how the good guy, meaning the right one for you, is never far away even if most of the time you don't realise it straight up. Then there's a first-person account from Simone, thirty-nine, explaining how Raymond, her ex-neighbour from across the landing, fell in love with her from day one. She didn't look at him at first, and now he's the man of her life. They're married with two kids. And that's how the story goes. They're happy because they look like Mr and Mrs Average and spend their only night out of the week at the supermarket.

For all I know, the perfect man I'm not even giving a second look, and who I'll have two kids with later, is Nabil . . . I gave him a hard time before. Said the guy was a pizza-face and things like that. But when I think about it, he helped me for months without getting anything in return, and most of all he had the guts to kiss me by surprise and risk getting kneed where it hurts. Bet if I asked Mrs Burlaud what she thinks, she'd tell me to give Nabil a chance. To be honest he's not a total neek. You could even call him one of the good guys. And another thing, acne doesn't last your whole life.

When he gets back from holiday, I'll talk to him for real. Not play the autistic kid like I do with everyone else to protect myself. For all I know, maybe I won't even need to say anything. It'll just happen, like in those romantic films where the leads don't talk to each other because they've just got this understanding. I hope it'll work out that way for Nabil and me. I'd suit me fine.

I haven't talked about it with Mum yet but I think she likes Nabil because the guy's ambitious, you get me. Like he wants to take part in *The Big Deal* on TV and win the car. I respect that because I'm no good at thinking about the future. I should go for Sherif's technique: he's been putting money on the horses for years and losing all the time, but he just keeps on going. Doesn't give a shit. Maybe that's the answer: always hold out hope and stop being scared of losing.

News about Samra has washed up on the estate. Samra's the prisoner who used to live in my block, the one with the brother and dad who pushed her so close to the edge she had to get out. Seems like somebody saw her a few days back, not so far away, or else very far away, I can't remember. Whatever, they're saying she ran away from home for a boy. The way I'm thinking, she didn't need a reason to want to escape from that prison. Word is she's fine. Met this guy at Toys R Us last December when she was working there for the holidays. She had a job wrapping up Christmas presents. I guess she got a good technique going, and that's what attracted her man who was working there too. Everyone's making out he's a *toubab*, as in white, a camembert, an aspirin you get me. So Samra's brother, the one with a boxing glove instead of a brain, wants this guy's skin even though the only crime he's committed is showing his sister a bit of love. I reckon they must of moved away, set up home further out so people leave them alone. They'll be in a hideout, like runaways, guilty of doing something normal. Seems like some people have to fight for everything. Even love.

Anyway, now that she's with the guy she loves, far away from that detention centre AKA her home, she can do what she wants. Basically, she's free. Well, more or less . . . It's just he'd better not dump her. If after they've been together for a year he suddenly decides to chuck all her belongings onto the landing and shout, 'Get out!' she wouldn't be able to do anything except leave, like a fool . . . She'd live in some skanky hotel room she'd pay for out of the money she earned ironing at the Farandole laundry. And most of all, she wouldn't believe in anything any more. Not men, or love.

My wisdom teeth are coming through. They're so painful. I'll have to go and see Mrs Atlan. Mrs Atlan's the dentist round here. Thing to remember is, don't be frightened of her. She's friendly and all that, but I reckon she picked up the job on the ground, like during the Gulf War or the Turkish invasions or I don't know what. Point is, she's kind of brutal this lady. Once, she nearly pulled out my whole jawbone. I was trying to shout, waving my arms around in her chair so she could get I was in pain, and she's like no worries. Just kept on going and said:

'Show us what you're made of, girl, come on, you can take it!'

Then, seeing like I was in *this* much pain, she tried to take my mind off it:

'D'you like couscous balls?'

When she was a teenager, it must of been a toss up between female wrestler, riot police-woman and dentist. It can't have been an easy decision, but she went for the job that combined violence with perversity. I guess it was more fun that way, for a psychopath like her.

I can really picture her at my age. Depressed teenager, kind of on-the-edge-masochist. Dressing like Action Man, listening to heavy metal to get to sleep at night and snacking on instant coffee granules. Then one day, she goes to buy some rice at the supermarket and falls in love with the old black American guy pictured on the orange box. He was called Uncle, this man, and his family name was Ben's. Old Ben's, he's been on that pack of rice since back in the day, so he must of been old for the longest time. For all we know, he's been dead for years and nobody knows. Maybe Uncle's rice company hid his death from the whole world because they didn't want to disappoint thousands of customers. Poor Uncle.

Could be he died alone in the middle of a rice-field, and nobody knew. Makes me think of the kid in the Kinder egg photo. Goes back twenty years, at least. That guy must be in his thirties now. A manager in a company making lavender air-freshener, married to a busty blonde, living in the US in one of those trendy suburbs where the houses all look the same. Swimming pool, SUV parked out front, and the dog that doesn't bite, yeah him again, all well behaved in his kennel with his name written above: Walker.

I wonder why they call them wisdom teeth ... The more they grow, the more you understand stuff? Personally, I've learned that learning hurts.

I'm telling you, it came out of nowhere. It was Sarah who told me. If she wasn't four years old, I'd of never believed her. I was reading one of Lila's magazines when she plonked herself in front of me, looked at me in an 'I-know-something-you-don't' kind of a way . . . and said:

'Dew-no-wot, Mummy's in love with that big man who's got not nice teeth.'

Lila and Hamoudi! I thought I was going to have an asthma attack. How could they of done that to me? I felt like I was in a Channel 1 report, in that *Seven to Eight* programme fronted by TV's brainy answer to Ken and Barbie.

It starts like this:

'Fifteen, and she already feels let down. Life's just a passing illusion for her. From the moment she is born, she's a massive disappointment to her parents, especially her father who knew what he was expecting to come out of his wife's belly: a little boy weighing in at three and a half kilos, measuring 50 centimetres, equipped with an average willy, perhaps to reinforce his own sense of virility.

'Sadly, it was not to be. He brought a little girl into the world and she was already wondering what on earth she was doing there . . .'

Then you see me appear on the screen, blurry-faced and with a disguised voice like in a cartoon. I turn to the camera and start pouring my heart out:

'Anyway, I mean, what's the point of living? I still haven't got any boobs, my favourite actor's gay, there's pointless wars and inequality between people and now the cherry on the cake: Hamoudi's sleeping with Lila and he hasn't even mentioned it to me. I know what I'm saying here, our lives are full of shit.'

Then the guy doing the voiceover picks up again, with all this tear-jerk music in the background.

'The kid's not wrong, our lives *are* full of shit. I think I'm going to stop doing telly voiceovers. It's a shitty job. You never get any recognition. And it's not like anyone ever asks for your autograph in the street, you don't get to be a celeb, it's a job for morons. I'll set up a group: Voiceovers Anonymous, because no one ever reads my name in the credits. I've had enough, I can't take it any more.

'But while I'm still on air, I'd like to take this opportunity to say I'm selling my car if anyone's interested. It's a green Twingo in good condition, practically new, only seven years old . . .'

And to find that out from Sarah. I mean, what's it going to be next? Why didn't Hamoudi say anything? Does he still take me for a kid? Maybe he thinks I don't understand these kinds of things? But I've managed to understand stuff a lot more complicated than that. Like, I've always done the paperwork for Mum. When my dad was around, it was still me who did it. Even when I'd had enough because tax forms are like gobbledygook. Once, I asked my dad how he and Mum managed before I could read and write. He thought I was being rude. Hit me. And not just a slap. He hit me long and hard. But I never cried. At least not in front of him. My dad was like Hamoudi's: he thought girls were weak, only good for crying and doing the washing-up.

It's good not all dads are like that. Take Nabil's. He's nice. He never hits him and he talks to him all the time. They even go out for walks together when the weather's nice. Plus Nabil's lucky: his parents are cultured, they can read and write and for his thirteenth birthday they bought him these wicked roller-blades, the kind I've dreamed about all my life. I used to cut them out of mail order catalogues at Christmas, so I could get a closer look.

Hamoudi just doesn't get it. I'm not a kid any more.

Mrs Burlaud's got a point: lots of things change over time. Sometimes, I think she should of gone into Chinese proverbs for a career. She was talking about Mum who's found a new job thanks to her training course. Mum looked so happy when she told me and it was the longest time since I'd seen that. The council took her on as a dinner lady. She dishes up for the kids at Jean-Moulin primary school. She's even got her name in pink on her overall: Yasmina.

There's just one problem: she has to serve pork in the canteen, specially on Tuesdays, and she reckons she's going to hell for it. Once, she told me a secret. Said the *haâlouf* didn't look so bad ... Made me laugh. But she blamed herself to death for daring to think that and for telling me.

I don't know what they did to her on that course but she's a different woman. She's happier, more radiant too. That's what they wrote about Céline

Dion in *Paris Match*, after the birth of her baby. Plus Mum's starting to get by in reading too. She can sound out the syllables pretty much correctly. She does this thing of stopping suddenly in the street to work out what's written on billboards or shop fronts. She went and bought a newspaper last time she was out. Yeah OK, so she just looked at the cartoons but it's a start. Even Cyborg Services pointed out to her she was making progress.

I mention her because she came round to the house the other day, kind of unexpected. She asked loads of questions about Mum's work, then started on about my career and my future in hairdressing. What did she expect? That faffing about with people's hair was my big passion in life? What a **** (I'm doing some censoring here). Her fancy biro definitely wasn't ticking the right boxes in our file with its twelve-digit serial number. She still hasn't clicked that I didn't actually have an alternative. At one point, the fool thought she was being clever, looked at me and said:

'It's too easy to let other people make your choices for you, Doria . . .'

That's when I did my Hollywood star turn. Stared straight at her, voice filled with emotion and a tear in my eye:

'Are you sure?'

That wrong-footed the robot. She couldn't think of anything more to say to me, so she started talking to Mum about the war in Iraq.

'It's always the women and children who suffer. Isn't war just horrible? Hmm . . . Right. By the way, I hear you've managed to pay the rent on time this month?'

I swanned off into the kitchen to clean the gas cooker before Cyborg did her inspection because it really was disgusting.

Maybe that's what I should do. Acting. You've got to admit, making films is classy. Fame, money, perks . . . I can already see myself at the Cannes Film Festival, dressed like Sissi, Empress of Austria in that cool film about her life, posing and smiling at the flock of photographers as their cameras flash. Waving casually at the crowd come to cheer me. No kidding. All those people would be there for me. Not for Nicole Kidman or Julia Roberts . . . Just for me. And there'd be Mum, all choked up, being interviewed for the TV channels: 'Iz so looong time I dream my dotter climb ze ladder at Cannes, iz marvillos, zank you viry much . . .' Not the ladder, Mum, the steps . . . While I'm walking up them, I'd be secretly hoping the ceremony would be broadcast on Moroccan television so as Mr How-Big-Is-My-Beard might just happen to catch it. He'd kick himself for leaving now his daughter's a star. Not a peasant woman. During the awards ceremony, I'd see my mum, Hamoudi, Lila who'd be pregnant by then, Sarah and Mrs Burlaud, all in the front row. Robert De Niro would call out my name to present me with the prize for best actress and slip his mobile phone number down the front of my low-cut dress while he was giving me a peck on the cheek. Everyone's on their feet. There I am, in front of them. Standing ovation! Luckily, I've seen it coming, written a brilliant speech. And, just to feel more at ease, more natural, more me if you like, I've learned it by heart:

' . . . and finally, I'd like to thank the Single Family Benefits Office in Seine-Saint-Denis for sponsoring my trip to Cannes. Thank you, dear public!'

OK, there's more, but I'm realising it might be better to stop daydreaming and put more energy into scrubbing this bloody gas cooker because it's filthy, you get me. They do my head in, thinking they can just drop by like this.

After she'd done her nice little inspection, our dear Cyborg Services left.

We thought that was it. Cut. Wrap for the day.

Everyone clear the set. But no. Fifteen minutes later she's back again, panting because she's legged it up the stairs – the lift's still out of order – and in a blind panic. Someone's just jacked the Opel Vectra she parked at the bottom of our block, she tells us. Can she call a taxi? Kind of surprised, Mum says: 'But our telephone iz cut off for two maybe three months.' I swear, you'd of thought that social worker had seen the devil. 'It's not written on your file . . .'

I saw Hamoudi the other evening and he told me about getting it together with Lila. I wanted to have a serious grown-up conversation about him not mentioning it . . . But in the end, I didn't dare. He looked so in love. I didn't want to break the spell. She was all he talked about for two whole hours. Lila's taken over from Rimbaud, you get me. Shown the poet the door. Go on, hop it . . . Like, he's even planning to take her on a weekend break with his drug-dealing money.

Plus he's started talking about fate. Yeah, that again. One thing's for sure, everything's linked to fate here. For better or worse. As for me, I'm realising fate doesn't like me so much, for the time being any way. Like Mrs Burlaud says, I haven't finished being disappointed yet. For an old lady, she's hasn't just got her eye on the ball, she's got it on the whole flipping pitch. I mean it: she said that to me even before the holidays started. What have I done? Spent my whole summer banging my head against a brick wall.

So seeing how I'd got nothing better to do, I decided to prepare myself psychologically for Nabil coming back. I was expecting something sensational, you get me, like *Nabil, The Return 2*. Yeah, right, Nabil's return. Neeky Nabil, AKA that fat dumpling.

I was thinking that when he got back, I'd be able to tell him how my feelings were all weird and muddled up inside me. Meaning I was ready, you get me. And then that acne-face of an idiot, he gets back from his holidays all tanned and, like, he doesn't even know me any more. Straight up. Ever since Nabil got back from Djerba, he doesn't rate me. Walks right past without saying hello. And another thing, he's got an earring and some bum-fluff on his chin. He's growing up, he's showing off, here we go.

Makes me think of *Grease* with Olivia Newton-John and John Travolta. It's summer, in their story. Olivia and Trav *like* each other, you get me. They run along the beach, sing happy songs and kiss on the lips over by the rocks. Then term starts again, and Olivia's still feeling the moment but Trav's got to show off in front of his crew at school, so he makes out he doesn't care because he's ashamed of her. He totally laughs in her face.

And like a fool, with her ponytail and pink dress, she runs off to bawl her eyes out. What a big girl's blouse. But the real bastard's Trav with his tight black leather trousers and bouffant hairdo. On Monday I told Mrs Burlaud the whole story about Nabil and she cheered me up no end. Without even meaning to.

'Maybe Nabil prefers boys. Had you thought about that?'

Oh yeah. Like Jarod. Maybe that's it. With a mother like his, he'd have to turn out gay wouldn't he? Probably knows all Kylie's songs by heart and wears super tight underwear.

Ffff . . . Whatever. Actually, Mrs Burlaud hasn't got a clue if Nabil's gay or not. All I know is I'm kind of disappointed because I thought he really liked me, that's all.

Our neighbour Rachida, AKA the biggest gossip on the estate, came round the other evening. She brought us thirty euros and some shopping for the week. From time to time, people from our area decide we're a needy cause, and it helps us out. But what's good with big Rachida is, as well as giving us her charity, she brings us 'Celebrity Gossip', the Paradise Estate Remix. We get all the latest news from her, and when she's got a specially juicy piece of information she's *this* proud of it like it's her first-born son.

Rachida talked to mum again about Samra, the prisoner from the eleventh floor who ran away from home to be with her guy. Turns out she's actually gone and married him.

Samra's dad's a retired torturer now (since his daughter's left). So he's buying a newspaper one morning when he happens to land on the 'Marriages' column, and there's his daughter's surname, meaning his too, next to this *toubab* guy's. Her old man couldn't take it and fell ill.

Word is part of his body's paralysed. From the shock of seeing his name 'dirtied' like that. The name carried by his father, his grandfather and others before them. Another question of honour, I guess.

Samra's dad's going to paralyse the other half of his body the day he happens to land on the 'Births' column. If he could put his pride to one side, he'd see the most important thing is his daughter's happiness. (I'm going into American TV moralising mode here, but I don't care, I'm taking a stand.)

And another thing, with all these stories about fate, I'm starting to think there's no such thing as coincidence.

It's all screwed up. It's not down to chance that the midget in that adventure game show *Fort Boyard* is actually a ticket inspector in real life and works for Paris Transport. You flip out the day you're fare-dodging at the Gare du Nord and some short-arse inspector asks to see your ticket. At first you can't see anybody in front of you, but then you look down and see the famous dwarf. Plus you know there's no point trying to leg it because the guy can run, I've watched him in the Fort. For all we know, maybe all the guys from the show work for the public sector.

I'm telling you, if they cut our TV off like they

did with the phone, that'd be too much. It's all I've got. When we did the Middle Ages with Mr Werbert, my geography teacher from last year, he told us how stained glass windows in churches were like the poor person's Bible, for people who couldn't read. I reckon these day's it's the TV that's the poor person's Koran.

When I watch the telly, Mum listens to Enrico Macias and knits. Oh yeah. Forgot to mention that. She's started knitting again. She used to do it loads before Dad left. Now, she knits at home with 'Jiklin', as in Jacqueline her teacher who she's got friendly with. Jacqueline was blonde before she went old and grey. Or that's what she told me. She sometimes makes rhubarb jam on a Sunday and her neighbours are football fans so she has problems getting to sleep on match evenings. She's nice, Jacqueline. Once, Mum told her she wished she had a vinyl cloth for the table, just like that, in the middle of a conversation, and the next week, Jacqueline brought this tablecloth round to the house. Yeah, OK, so it was bare ugly, there were these hunting scenes, with big stags and a load of bambis getting shot at . . . But I thought it was nice of her, all the same.

And another thing, Jacqueline's interested in

tons of stuff. She asks Mum questions about religion, Moroccan culture and lots of things like that . . . 'It's so I know if it's true, what they're saying on the telly . . . '

And sometimes she tells Mum stories from the Bible. The other day, she told her the story of Job. I remember this time we had to read out a bit of that story in our literature lesson with Mrs Jacques. She shouted at me because when it was my turn to read, instead of pronouncing it Job-rhymes-with-globe, I said 'Djob'. Like the English word for work. And that crazy old bag accused me of 'sullying our beautiful literature' and other moronic stuff. Wasn't my fault. I didn't even know this Job guy existed. 'It's because of PEOPLE-LIKE-YOU that our Frrrench herrrritttage is in a coma!'

Thanks to Lila, Hamoudi's come through his bad patch. He's got a new job: security at Malistar, the mini-market underneath our block. Just while he's waiting to find something else and to quit dealing for good. He's smoking a lot less. We're seeing each other less too. But he's doing better, and that's what matters. Before, he was always saying how it was all fucked anyway, there was no way out. But when he said that, he'd always apologise straight after.

'I've got no right to say stuff like that to a fifteen-year-old kid. Don't listen to me, all right? You've got to keep believing, OK?

It was almost like he was threatening me. But he was right. Today, he's found his emergency exit. Like, he's seriously talking about making a life with Lila. Meaning there isn't just rap and football. Love's another way out.

'I've got no right to say - and like - and to a
literary career, but I don't believe so, all right.
You've got to keep believing, O.'

It was almost like he was threatening me. But
he was right. Indeed, he's found his encouragement. Like he's personally telling those that are
his with Luke. Perhaps that's the upshot up, and
hopeful to a certain degree too.

The first day back has to be one of the worst in the whole year. That and Christmas. I had diarrhoea for three days before. The idea of going to a new school you don't know, with loads of people you don't know and, worse, who don't know you, well it gives me the squits. Sorry, butterflies. Sounds less disgusting.

Louis-Blanc Secondary School. So who is he anyway, this Louis Blanc? I looked it up in the *Petit Robert* dictionary of proper names. With a name like that, he's got to be in there.

'Louis BLANC (1811–1882). Journalist, socialist, activist.'

In France, all you need are three words ending in 'ist' for you to get a school, a street, a library or a Metro station named after you. I thought it might be a good idea to gen up a bit. You never know, some wanker might just ask me: 'Oi, you! Who's Louis Blanc?' And I'd be able to look the bastard straight in the eye and say: 'Journalist, socialist, activist . . .' And with an American accent too, like in those undubbed films we used to watch in English class. That's shut you up, hasn't it? Even if you're not circumcised, *fool.*

The morning of the first day back, Mum was so sweet. She wanted her daughter to be the most beautiful for 'Ze new zkooll, the *jdida . . . Hamdoullah.*' She ironed my least ugly clothes, specially the fake Levi's jeans (very good imitation) she got for me at La Courneuve market. 'It's all got to go, innit! Miss . . . Sir . . . You can't afford not to. Levi's jeans at twelve euros we're *giving* them away. They're seventy in the shops! It's all got to go, innit!' She spent ages doing my long black hair. Just like hers when she was younger. But when she started getting old, some of it fell out and it wasn't totally black any more. She brushed olive oil into my hair then did it up in a ponytail. We're talking old-skool hairdressing. Like back in the *bled.* I wasn't so big on it myself, but I didn't say anything to her because she was so happy making me all pretty. It reminded me of those mornings we had the class photos at primary school, and she used to do the same thing. My hair looked all silky and shiny in the photos, like in the Schwarzkopf ads: 'Professional HairCare *for you.*' But actually, it was full of Zit Zitoun olive oil, and smelled of fry-ups. When the teacher patted me on the head for giving a good answer, she used to wipe her hands on her jeans. On class photo day, all the teachers wore jeans.

Who cares. As long as I was pretty in Mum's eyes. It makes me proud when people say I look like her. I hardly look like my dad at all. Except for my eyes, which are green like his. There was always this sort of far-away look in my dad's eyes. So when I stand in front of the mirror, I can't help seeing him and his far-away look. All the time. Mrs Burlaud told me I'd be completely cured the day I see me in the mirror. Just me.

Mum lined my eyes with kohl so as to make them stand out. She kissed me on the forehead and closed the door behind me calling on God to go with me. Hope he's got his own wheels because public transport stresses me out. I walked down to the town hall to catch the bus to Louis-Blanc. And who do I see in the bus, stretched out across the four seats at the back, Walkman jammed into his ears? Neeky Nabil. What a coincidence.

He catches my eye and does this guy-feeling-guilty face like they do in the movies. 'Awigh?' he asks with this quick nod, so quiet you can barely hear him. So now he's being a lazybones too. Letters like L and R and T too difficult to pronounce? My answer's to screw up my eyes and pinch my lips really tight, meaning: 'Fuck you, Nabil AKA the fat dumpling, you pizza-faced microbe, homosexual and total ego-trip.' Hope he knew how to translate all that.

Then I went and sat next to an old African man holding this wooden rosary in his hand. He was slipping the beads slowly through his fingers. Reminded me of my dad in his rare moments of piety, even if there was no way you could call him a good Muslim. You don't pray after demolishing a pack of Kronenburg 1664. No point.

So anyway, Nabil got out three stops before me. Didn't say goodbye, see you, *beslama*. Nothing, *walou*. The 'Awigh?' must of taken it out of him. If you can't say 'All right?', 'Goodbye' is really going to be asking too much. Got to fess up, I was kind of full of rage inside. But the worst was still to come.

I get to Louis-Blanc-out-of-a-dictionary Technical College and find myself in the middle of thirty peroxide slags with big fat perms, and it's like *liberty, equality, fraternity* eat your heart out. It didn't look like the start of the new school year. More like some casting for a photo shoot. They were all fashion-victim trendy, this season's 'look'. So, with my kohl eyeliner and fake jeans, I was feeling a bit out of it.

Then they called us out by group to go to our classrooms. The head teacher's a woman. She's called Agnès Bernard, but she's got nothing to do with Agnès B. She's a young teacher who's probably not quite thirty, blonde, talks with a lisp and dresses like everyone else. Yeah, ordinary. Lucky for her she's got that lisp, or else there'd be nothing original about her at all, poor thing. She explained what the hairdressing course involved and what the hell we were going to be doing all year. 'Product technology: regulations concerning personal hygiene products,

primary ingredients used in hair-care products
... Equipment technology: instruments for drying and styling the hair, cutting tools and implements, styling accessories ... Professional techniques, of course: shampooing, bleaching, dyeing, perms, drying, setting ...' Chinese, you get me. Gobbledygook. What the hell was I doing in that place?

By the time I got back home, I was seriously depressed. I don't like bursting into tears but I couldn't help myself. I was hardly through the front door when I started blubbing. It was this close whether I'd set off an emergency flood alert in the building. Luckily Mum wasn't there. I know what she's like, and she'd of started blubbing too without even knowing why I was blubbing.

A few days later, I stopped babysitting. Too busy, doing loads of stuff. Totally over-booked. No more time to look after a kid. Sorry. No can do.

Nah, I don't look after Sarah any more because Hamoudi's doing it instead of me. Seeing how he works on the estate and finishes at four o'clock, he can pick her up. It's cool. Yeah. Plus it makes them look like a proper family.

I see Hamoudi when I go to do the shopping downstairs. He talks to me in front of Malistar while he's unloading boxes of rice. After about five minutes I feel I'm getting in his way, so I head off. To be honest, he talks to me the same way he does everybody else. He's no longer Hamoudi of Hallway 32. And he knows it. The other day, I found a note in our mail box, along with twenty euros. It was signed 'Moudi'. A nickname. A crap nickname. Even I'd of come up with something better. When I think how Hamoudi used to say nicknames were bare stupid. And now here he is signing off 'Moudi'. How come Lila didn't find something else. Moudi. Moody . . . schmoody . . . what? Doesn't mean anything, doesn't say anything. Nicknames are *so* smug-married: 'D'you want some more duck, my little rabbit?' Works the other way round too. How sad is that?

So anyway, because he was giving himself a hard time for dropping me and because he wanted to clear his conscience, he put this note in the letterbox along with twenty euros. He thinks money can plug a gap, or what? Plus he's got to stop reading the psycho-babble in those women's magazines on Lila's coffee table. Even what he wrote was rubbish: 'If you need me, you know where to find me . . .' Yeah, well what I know Hamoudi is you're never in Hallway 32 any more. You've dropped us, Rimbaud and me. You lightweight. They're all the same. They all drop you in the end.

If she wasn't paid to see me at a fixed time once a week, I bet even Mrs Burlaud would of dropped me by now.

Walking past the newsagent's on the main shopping street, I noticed a bit of paper stuck up in the window. It said: 'LOTTERY WINNER HERE: 65, 000 euros'. OK so there's always a LOTTERY WINNER. But they never put who it is. The guys behind the counter at the newsagent's aren't snitches, you get me, they're safe. They'd never grass up a winner. Except this time I know who the jammy bastard is. Our very own international Sherif. Bet he goes on TV and becomes a celebrity. That way, he'll get round the identity checks. Yeah, if he's famous, they won't stop him and ask for his name any more. Come on, he deserved it. He's been trying long enough. I'm curious to find out what he'll do with the money. Change his baseball cap? Jeans? Flat? Estate? Country? Maybe he'll buy a villa in Tunis, settle down over there and find himself a wife who makes couscous like a pro . . .

Talking about marriage, I grilled my mum on it. Turns out she likes the mayor of Paris. Yeah, she's been in love with Bertrand Delanoë ever since she saw him on telly laying the memorial plaque at Saint-Michel. It was in honour of the Algerians who were thrown into the Seine during the demonstration on 17 October 1961. I borrowed books about it from Livry-Gargan library.

Mum thought it was big of Bertrand to do something in memory of the Algerian people. Very dignified, very classy. Now she's single, I'm thinking of bringing her to Mr Delanoë's attention. Big poster campaign with Mum's photo (that black and white one in her passport) and the slogan: 'You get my vote Mr Mayor, *call me.*' It'll drive Bertrand wild if he sees the poster. I reckon he's single too. Yeah, you never see him flaunting it with chicks. Plus with mum, it's like when Sherif lays a bet: 'There's everything to play for.' She cooks, she cleans, she even knits. Bet nobody's ever knitted a pair of woollen underpants dedicated to 'Dear Mayor, it's with great pleasure that . . .' He'll be so happy in winter.

The other evening, I ran into Hamoudi by the recycling bins. He told me I was just the person he was looking for. Pffffff. Like I believe that. I could see he was headed for Lila's.

'Hamoudi, you big fat liar!'

No, I didn't say that actually. I just went: 'Oh,

really . . .?' We talked for a bit. He told me he was sorry he's not around as much as he used to be . . . Big picture is, he made me understand he's got a new life now and I also got the message I wasn't really part of it any more.

'Hamoudi, I liked you better when you were a hoodlum and you stuck your fingers up to the police.'

No, I didn't really say that either. Just went: 'Yeah, all right.'

Him and Lila are even thinking of getting married. She must be happy, Hamoudi's mum I mean. Managing to get all her children married off like that. 'You've reached the top level. Bonus score. You're a winner!' Fatima's fulfilled her mission. Plus it's good timing. Twenty-eight's fine. He's got in just before those questions start popping up in his mum's mind . . . 'Allah, my God, perhaps my son he iz a . . . maggot?! *Hchouma* . . .'

Hamoudi'd better invite me to his wedding. If he doesn't, I'll squeal on him . . . No, only joking. That'd be going too far. There's this guy in the area turned his crew in to the police. Been persecuted ever since and gets called a *harki* like those Algerians who fought for France. I'd never go that low. Poor guy, for as long as he lives on the

Paradise estate he'll be tagged a traitor. Round here, you do one thing that's not so well viewed and it's all over. You get pigeon-holed to death.

Which reminds me of what happened to a girl who lived round here a few years back. It made the newspaper. She was a good student, everybody in the neighbourhood respected her family, and the really tough kids would help her dad with his shopping bags when he came back from the market on Sunday mornings. This girl was in a theatre group funded by Livry-Gargan council and her parents were cool about it. Sometimes, they even went to see her performing in the end of year show. So basically, things weren't going too badly for her at all, even if her parents thought her acting was just a hobby, like Wednesday afternoon Painting Club when you're in Big Class at nursery school. Thing is, she really liked acting and wanted to make a career out of it. When she was eighteen, she even did a tour of France with her company.

Then one day, her parents found an anonymous note in their box. That anti-racist newspaper *Friend to Friend* published a first-person account by this girl and quoted the whole letter:

Your daughter keeps the wrong kind of company, she goes out too much and is frequently seen

walking with boys. We've heard things about her that taint your name and reputation. The neighbourhood knows that **** spends time with young men and that she is forgetting the right path. God says that you are responsible for the path of your children. You must be strict with her so that she fears her family and the religion of Islam. Now people can see that your daughter is on the street and she is not afraid. The French are taking her with them on the road to evil. It has come to our notice that she wears make-up and dyes her hair. This means she likes to please men and that she is tempting Satan. If something shameful happens, God can see you have been too free with her and you are as much to blame as she is.

With God's mercy and forgiveness, she can return to the family and to our customs if you adopt strict measures. Prayer is God's way of helping she who turns away from the path.

Your family is one that we respect and it must continue that way. A girl can be led on the right path by her father. You must believe in the power God gives you to be a good family.

After the letter, everything changed for this girl. The anonymous bastard who wrote all those stupid things managed to convince her parents.

They felt guilty for giving their daughter 'too much' freedom. So all of a sudden, she wasn't allowed to do her theatre group any more, or to go out, not even to buy a loaf of bread. But most of all, she kept hearing talk of marriage. That's the last resort when parents sense their daughters are slipping through their fingers.

In *Friend to Friend*, she talked about how she decided to run away from home. Now she lives on her own and doesn't really have any contact with her parents. But she's working as an actress with the Comédie Française and she's earning a living doing what she loves. So in spite of everything, she's won.

It's happened. I'm sixteen. I've seen sixteen springs, like they say in the movies. Nobody remembered. Not even Mum. No one wished me a happy birthday this year. They didn't last year either. Sorry, last year I got an order form from Agnès B with a special free gift if I sent back the 'Agnès B wishes you a happy birthday' voucher within ten days. But this year, nothing. Agnès B's got it in for me. We're talking *this* mad because I didn't send her shitty voucher back. Fool. It's not like I care. Anyway, those gifts are always bigger in the photo than in real life.

Too bad if no one's remembered my birthday this year.

To be honest, I kind of understand. It's not like I'm anyone out of the ordinary. Some people, everyone remembers their birthday. They might even get a mention in the newspaper. But me, I'm nobody. It's not as if I know how to do much either. Well, a few things, but nothing special, you get me: I can crack my toe bones, propel a sliver of saliva out of my mouth and suck it back in again, do an Italian accent in front of the bathroom mirror in the morning. Yeah, I can get by as it happens. But if I was a boy, maybe it'd be different. Matter of fact, I bet it'd be different.

For a start, my dad would still be here. Rather than in Morocco. And then for Christmas 1994, I'd of got Fisher Price roller-blades and a reply to the letter I sent Father Christmas. Yeah, it'd all of gone better if I'd been a boy. I'd have loads of photos of me as a little kid, like Sarah does. My dad would of taught me to chew tobacco, told me a pile of smutty stories he'd picked up on building sites and plus, from time to time, he'd of patted me on the shoulder, a sort of bonding thing, like: 'You're the best!' Yeah, yeah. I'd of even had fun scratching lots between my legs to prove my manliness. I'd have no problem being a boy. But what can you do, I'm a girl. A babe. A chick. I'll get used to it in the end.

The other day, Mum and me went to the Taxiphone in the square to call Aunt Zohra. They're popping up everywhere, these Taxiphones. What with their wooden booths, glass doors and that phone number on the handset, they really make me think of the home country. Basically, the whole Taxiphone idea is *made in the bled.* The one in the square is a small piece of Oujda in Livry-Gargan.

Aunt Zohra's doing OK. She's promised to come and visit us soon. And she said that Youssef would be out in May. It sounded definite because she didn't say '*insh'Allah*'. Seems like she recognises him less with each visit. She told Mum he's started ranting in this hardcore way, worse than his dad. I'm thinking, if that's who she's comparing him to, it must be bad.

I guess he's met some weird people in there. Youssef always used to be easy-going, plus he was loads more open than most guys his age. These days, he talks about sin and divine retribution.

Before, he wasn't so bothered about all that. He'd even go and buy bacon-flavoured crisps on the sly just to find out what they tasted like. I think it's dodgy, a sudden change like that. Someone must of taken advantage of him being vulnerable in prison and inserted some big fat disks into his brain. I can't wait for May so he gets out.

As far as good news goes, I flicked on to this regional report on France 3 the other evening and who do I see on the telly, looking all nice in her pink *boubou* dress? Fatouma Konaré, my mum's ex-colleague from the Formula 1 in Bagnolet. Her name was up on the screen with, underneath it: 'Union delegate'. The commentary was saying how the girls had won their battle. Their demands would shortly be met. Even the employees who got fired during the strike period or those who left without any compensation are going to see reparations. Does that mean Mum'll get some money too, even if she didn't go on strike? Straight off, I started thinking about that tosser Mr Schmidt. He must of been totally out of his depth! Ha ha ha! Nice one.

There you go, that'll do for my birthday present, knowing there is some justice in this world after all. I was starting to have serious doubts. I was fed up of always hearing: 'The wheel will come full circle'. Couldn't see what wheel they were talking about, plus it's a stupid expression anyway.

To be honest, with all the things that've happened this year, I was thinking how life is too unfair. But recently, I've started to change my mind ... Loads of stuff's happened to change the way I look at things. That guy who was wrongly imprisoned getting to appear on *Everybody's Talking About It*. The cleaners' situation at the Formula 1 in Bagnolet. Hamoudi and Lila getting married next April. And lastly, the way Mum's changed since last year. It's seeing her getting better every day, fighting to provide for both of us that's made me start thinking it'll all work out in the end and maybe I've got to follow her example.

On the work front, I'm taking after her because there's no let-up from hairdressing. You dry, you style, and when you've finished, well, you just have to start all over again. No break. Even God had a rest on the seventh day. It's not normal. The one thing that comforts me is knowing I'm coping all right with school this year. Mind you, if I'd been useless at hairdressing, then I really would of been worried.

Mrs Burlaud told me my therapy was finished. I asked if she was sure. She laughed. That means I'm all right. Or else she's had enough of my stories. She must be flipping her lid with everything I tell her.

I'm glad it's stopping because there were a few things about her that bugged me. Her name, for starters . . . Burlaud, I mean come off it, what kind of a name is that, plus it sounds ugly. Then there's her perfume that stinks of Quit Nits shampoo and those jarring tests meant to reveal stuff about me . . . And another thing, she's old. Like, from another time frame. I see it when I'm talking to her. I have to think twice about everything I'm saying. Can't say a single word in slang or young people's language, even if that's the best way of getting her to understand how I'm feeling . . . When I can't find the proper phrase and I say something like 'oh my days' or 'bare', she takes it to mean something else or she does her *spesh* face. Doing her *spesh* face means looking like a total

165

idiot, because *spesh* (special) classes at primary school were for the most behind kids, the ones with the biggest problems. So you say *spesh* for someone who's a bit thick, you get me.

There you go, Mrs Burlaud and me weren't always on the same wavelength. Still, I know it's thanks to all that stuff I'm doing better now. So I'm not saying she didn't help me big time. I even said thank you to Mrs Burlaud, by the way. A real thank you.

But as we were leaving, she said something strange: 'Good luck!' I'd got used to hearing 'See you next Monday!' But this time, she said 'Good luck.' It was like the first time I rode a bike without stabilisers.

Youssef had lent me his bike. He told me he'd push while I was pedalling, but then there was this moment when he suddenly said out of the blue: 'I've let go!' His voice was far away. He'd let go a while back. And I carried on pedalling. Mrs Burlaud's 'Good luck' had the same effect on me as Youssef's 'I've let go!' It's happened, she's let me go.

On my way out, I felt like in the scene-before-the-end in a film, when the main characters have mostly solved the problem and it's time for a conclusion. Except for me, my conclusion's going to be longer and harder than *Jurassic Park.*

I still don't know what I really want to do because hairdressing, well let's say it's something you do while you're waiting for something else to come along. A bit like Christian Morin. He presented *The Wheel of Fortune* for years, but his real vocation was playing the clarinet.

Yesterday, I got an unexpected visit. Neeky Nabil came round while Mum was out. I opened the door. There he was, leaning against the wall, clean-shaven and smelling of cologne. He took off his baseball cap, smiled at me and said:

'Hi there, all right?'

I spent an age staring at him and not saying anything. I was as gob-smacked as those people who win the annual lottery draw for Casino super-markets. Then, after thinking about it for a bit, I decided I might as well let him in. We went to sit down and we got talking. About his holidays in Djerba, the last book he'd read, the start of his final year at school . . . He explained how he sat his baccalaureate last year but didn't pass. Obviously, it was a total nightmare for his mum, much more than for him. That ***** (another bit of self-censoring) told him he was spending too much time round at mine helping me out. Supposedly that's what stopped him doing his own work and revising for his exams. So it's my fault now?

Yeah, we really talked about everything. Even about . . . that thing I was kind of embarrassed about. You know what.

Nabil said he was sorry he kissed me without asking and that he hoped it hadn't upset me too much. I said no. So he did it again. Except this time it was better, like he knew what he was doing. Must of been practising at his holiday camp in Djerba with some seventeen-year-old German tourist on holiday with her journalist parents who worked for the Bavarian tabloid press. Bet she was blonde and called Petra, with green eyes and massive boobs.

Anyway, he didn't clear off afterwards. We watched the TV, him and me, and went on talking. He was even stroking my hair (luckily I hadn't put on any Zit Zitoun). I told him loads of things about me, my family and other stuff he didn't know . . . I told him about Hamoudi and how he used to recite Rimbaud's poems to me in Hallway 32. That's when Nabil surprised me again. He starts giving up 'The Orphans' New Year Gifts' by heart and he didn't stop as much as Hamoudi, no, he was really belting it out. It was nice. Except at the end, he kind of spoilt it all by looking at me with this sly smile and going: 'Impressed, huh?' I said no, and that made him laugh. So there you go, I've made it up with Nabil and I reckon . . . I like him. He's meant to be taking me to the cinema on Wednesday. I'm over happy. Last time was with school to see *The Lion King*.

I ran into Hamoudi, Lila and Sarah again this weekend. I was going to the shopping centre for Mum when they honked their horn at me. Took me a while to turn round and realise they meant *me*. Matter of fact, I never normally turn round when I hear a horn or someone whistling because it's always for the fat slag behind me in her strappy pink top and tight jeans. But this time, there wasn't a fat slag. So I got in and we all went to the shopping centre together.

Talk about happy families. I can see now, this is the best thing that's happened to Hamoudi since I've known him. I also noticed Hamoudi's changed car again. It was a red Opel Vectra this time. Exactly the same as the one our social worker got jacked from the parking area below our flat. But I didn't say anything.

Talking of Cyborg Services, she's been transferred to somewhere on the Atlantic coast because Mrs Wotsit's back from maternity leave.

She finally gave birth to her shrimp. Of course she made sure to bring all her sprog photos when she came to see us. So we were lucky enough to see Lindsay (yep, that's what she's called her . . . no comment) still covered in placenta in her mum's arms (don't know how Wotsit managed it, but her blow-dry was still looking perfect after the birth), Lindsay in the bath, Lindsay with her dad on the Ikea sofa, Lindsay going to sleepy-byes in her cradle, Lindsay having so many adventures you'd think she was bloody Tintin. Our Model Academy social worker looked chuffed to bits with her little Lindsay, who's on track to star in the Pampers ads a few months from now.

Mrs Thingumyjig's noticed a 'definite change' round at ours. She said she'd try and squeeze a bit more money out of the social services so we can go on holiday next summer, probably to the sea. Well . . . what can I say? Maybe Mrs Wotsit's actually the secret daughter of Mother Teresa and St Francis of Assisi. Generosity personified . . . Suddenly, I liked our dearly beloved social worker. A beach holiday! Oh my days . . . I take back everything I said about you, your husband and little Thingumyjig. Maybe you're nice after all.

* * *

So anyway, getting back to Hamoudi and Lila, while we were out shopping together, they talked some more to me about their marriage. They both want a traditional wedding. It's kind of weird, I wouldn't of expected it. But at least Lila's parents'll be pleased. She told me she'd patched things up with them just a few days back, after them not speaking for five years, basically since the day Lila decided to marry Sarah's dad. Then there's Hamoudi's mum who's shouting from the top of all the tower blocks on the estate that her youngest son's getting married. According to Rachida (always a reliable source), lots of people are viewing the marriage badly because Lila's a divorcee and she's already had a child with a white guy. But as for the soon-to-be-newly-weds, they don't give a shit. It's just a detail.

While Lila was trying on shoes in Bata, I gave Hamoudi the low-down on Nabil. He looked really happy for me, like something amazing had happened. I was hoping he'd react that way. Hamoudi's not the type to jump to conclusions and think that, if a girl's seeing a boy, it makes her a ****. Well, you get me.

'So, you're trying to beat us to it and get married first? Is he good-looking, this Nabil of yours? I bet I know him, if he grew up round here.'

'He's got big ears, but he's kind and clever and . . .'

'OK, that's it, you're in deep . . . No more "*kif-kif* tomorrow*", the way you complained back in the day . . . ?'

He was right. I'd nearly forgotten. But Hamoudi remembered. When he said that, I was this close to shedding a tear. It's what I used to say when I was down, and Mum and me were all on our own: '*kif-kif* tomorrow'. Nothing changes, today's just like tomorrow.

But now I'd say it differently. I'd say I just *like* tomorrow. Yeah, I'd give that ratings. It's more me. (Plus it's the kind of thing Nabil would say . . .)

Maybe there's something to that idea of the wheel turning, after all. Maybe it really *does* turn. And maybe it's not such a big deal if Jarod from *The Pretender* is gay, because Nabil told me Rimbaud was too . . . And maybe it's not such a big deal if I haven't got my dad any more, because there are loads of people out there who haven't got dads either. And anyway, I've got a mum.

She's doing better, by the way. She's independent, she can read and write (or nearly) and she didn't even go through therapy to get sorted. All she needs is a subscription to *Elle* and she'll be a real lady. What else could I ask for? You thought I was going to say 'nothing'? Well think again, because there's bare stuff I still haven't got. Loads of things that need changing round here . . . Hold on, now there's an idea. Why not go into politics? '*From highlights to high office: it's closer than you think* . . .' That's a slogan that sticks in your head. I'll have to think up some more along those lines. You know, the kind of quotes you read in history books at school, like that joker Napoleon saying: 'Every conquered nation needs a revolution.'

I'll lead the uprising on the Paradise estate. I

can see the newspaper headlines now: 'Doria sparks off the suburbs' or 'Militant heroine lights the urban fuse' But I wouldn't want a violent uprising, like in that film *La Haine* which doesn't exactly end happily-ever-after. It'll be a smart revolution with nobody getting hurt, and we'll all rise up to make ourselves heard. Life isn't just about rap and football. We'll be like the poet Rimbaud, fired up by 'the sobbing of the Oppressed, the clamour of the Cursed'.

I shouldn't spend so much time with Nabil. I'm getting way too political.

Glossary

babouches   North African slippers made of chamois leather and often decorated with sequins.

beslama   Goodbye.

bled   For North Africans, this refers to the homeland or mother country (originally meaning the North African interior). In metropolitan French, the term denotes a godforsaken place in the middle of nowhere.

boubou   A traditional West African dress.

haâlouf   Pig (and therefore not *hallal* but *haram* or forbidden food to Muslims).

hamdoullah   Thanks be to God.

harki   The Harkis were Algerians based in Algeria but who fought on the side of the French in the Algerian War of Independence (1954–1962).

hchouma   Disgrace, modesty, taboo, sexual shame which finds an old-fashioned parallel in the English concept of prudishness.

Insh'Allah   God willing, if Allah wills it so.

kif-kif   *Kif*, meaning hash or marijuana,

derives from the Arabic *kaif* for well-being and good humour. 'C'est du kif' meaning 'it's the same thing', is a related phrase with its origin in the term *kif-kif,* or 'more of the same', brought back to France by soldiers who served in North Africa at the end of the nineteenth century. Faïza Guène's original title, *Kiffe kiffe demain,* plays on both the downbeat sense of *kif-kif* and the enthusiasm behind *kiffer,* a contemporary 'street' verb meaning to feel high or to fancy somebody. *Kiffer* is hybrid French, the *k* giving it a deliberately Arabic feel. So Guène's title means both 'different day, same shit' and 'perhaps I might just *like* tomorrow'.

Maghrébines	North African women. In Arabic, 'the Maghreb' means the place where the sun sets. This contrasts with the French origin of the term 'the Levant', meaning the place where the sun rises.
Mektoub	What is written, the will of Allah; and hence fate, luck or destiny.
Merguez	A spicy North African sausage made from lamb, popular in France.
toubab	A white French person (originally from the Senegalese *Wolof* language), and more generally used by non-

whites. The word is playful and finds its counterpart in, say, the term '*beur*', for a non-white French person of North African origin. There is even a work of dark fiction by the French novelist, Jean-Claude Derey, entitled *Toubab or not Toubab.*

A Note on the Slang

Doria peppers her language with choice words from French *Verlan* or 'backslang'. This involves splicing and reversing words so that, for example, the French term *à l'envers* (meaning backwards, upside down or the wrong side up) becomes *verlan*. *Verlan* is the playful and defiant language of France's high-rise suburbs with their large immigrant communities. Although there's an improvised aspect to the word-play, it also has enough of a system for words to filter on through to the mainstream. This explains why words like *beur*, which is the backslang for *arabe* (used to refer to a second or third generation French national of North African origin) has been flipped again by those wordsmiths ahead of the game to form *rebeu*. Incidentally, *beur* is now viewed as a politically correct and non-inflammatory term.

Although we do have examples of backslang in English, there is no direct equivalent of *Verlan*. Where possible I have tried to find parallels and resonances in contemporary British urban slang, with all its multicultural influences. Examples might be 'oh my days' to register shock or wonder; 'bare' or 'over' meaning 'very'; 'safe' or 'heavy' to refer to something positively; or 'buff' meaning 'good-looking'. Sadly, I never got a chance to use 'minging' for 'no good'.